COMICAL MANIA!

Are you a funnies fan? A cartoon connoisseur? A comic book bug? Bring back that Saturday morning magic with crazy quizzes on everything from Archie to Alvin and the Chipmunks, from Batman to Bloom County, from Superman to Super Chicken! Start now with these trial teasers:

— What is Buck Rogers's real first name?
— Where does Fred Flintstone work?
— Did Beetle Bailey enlist or was he drafted?
— Which comic strip was never turned into a Broadway musical:
    a. Li'l Abner
    b. Annie
    c. Pogo
    d. Peanuts
— Casper the Friendly Ghost frolicked with which witch?
— Which came first, in print: Wizard of Id or B.C.?
— What's Daffy Duck's usual closing line?
— Where did Clark Kent attend college?
— What is the name of Thor's enchanted hammer?
— Name Bugs Bunny's girlfriend.

For the answers to these and more than a thousand other fascinating questions, keep on reading and surrender yourself to TRIVIA MANIA!

TRIVIA MANIA
by Xavier Einstein

TRIVIA MANIA has arrived! With enough questions to answer every trivia buff's dreams, TRIVIA MANIA covers it all—from the delightfully obscure to the <u>seemingly obvious</u>. Tickle your fancy, and test your memory!

COMICS & CARTOONS

TRIVIA Mania

BY XAVIER EINSTEIN

ZEBRA BOOKS
KENSINGTON PUBLISHING CORP.

The quiz master would like to thank the following people without whom this book would be vastly inferior: Len Wein, Marv Wolfman, Howard Weinstein, Dave McDonnell, Joey Cavalieri, Neal Pozner, Peter J. Sanderson, Judy Steingart, Matthew Novet. Finally, this volume is dedicated, with love, to a wonderful couple, Robert and Deborah Greenberger.

ZEBRA BOOKS

are published by

Kensington Publishing Corp.
475 Park Avenue South
New York, N.Y. 10016

First printing: August, 1984

Printed in the United States of America

TRIVIA MANIA:
Comics & Cartoons

1) Other than Road Runner, which Warner Bros. character did Wile E. Coyote confront?

2) What is the name of Cosmo Fishhawk's barber in *Shoe*?

3) Name two famous cartoon magpies.

4) Which is Zippy the Pinhead's favorite saying?
   a. Yow!
   b. Wowie!
   c. Sockamagee!
   d. Golly Geewhiz!

5) Which two members of Alpha Flight rose from the ranks of Gamma and Beta Flights in the Marvel comics?

6) Name the astronaut son of J. Jonah Jameson, Spider-Man's most outspoken critic.

. . . Answers

1. Bugs Bunny

2. Sal

3. Heckle and Jeckle

4. a

5. Puck and Marrina

6. John Jameson

7) Can you give the full names of the animated duo, Fox and Crow?

8) The aircraft carrier Enterprise selected which cartoon hero for its official mascot?

9) How did Ricochet Rabbit introduce himself?

10) Which of Beetle Bailey's buddies could get *anything*?

11) Who is the oldest child in *Family Circus*?

12) Who was the comic book fashion model who wore designs sent in by readers?

13) The Red Tornado is a man with vortex abilities. True or False?

14) Did the Beatles provide the voices for their cartoon series?

15) In *For Better or For Worse*, what part-time job does Ellie have?

16) How does Zatanna perform her magic in DC comics?

17) Name all the members of Top Cat's gang.

18) Whom does *Bloom County's* Cutter John date?

. . . Answers

7. Fauntleroy F. Fox and Crawford C. Crow

8. Atom Ant

9. "I'm Sheriff Bing-Bing-Bing! Ricochet Rabbit!"

10. Cosmo

11. Billy

12. Katy Keene

13. False, he's an android

14. No

15. She works in a library

16. She says her spells backward

17. Benny the Ball, the Spook, Brain, Choo Choo, Fancy Fancy

18. Bobbi Harlow

19) Are Wonder Woman and Wonder Girl related?

20) *Mad's* Sergio Aragones has created a bumbling barbarian. What is his name?

21) Before *Prince Valiant*, Hal Foster illustrated which strip?
   a. Buck Rogers
   b. Jungle Jim
   c. Tarzan
   d. Terry and the Pirates

22) What could Underdog do if he were in dire trouble?

23) Name the blind sculptress in love with the *Fantastic Four's* Thing.

24) Roy Harper is the former ward of which DC superhero?

25) Mighty Manfred the Wonder Dog was companion to which cartoon hero?

26) Voice master Mel Blanc hates carrots. True or False?

27) Which Vietnamese terrorist is now a UN delegate in *Doonesbury*?

. . . *Answers*

19. No

20. Groo the Wanderer

21. c

22. Take the pill hidden in his ring for extra strength

23. Alicia Masters

24. Oliver Queen, the Green Arrow

25. Tom Terrific

26. True

27. Phred

28) Zonker Harris has nightmares about which sports figure?
- a. Mark Spitz
- b. Bruce Jenner
- c. Wilt Chamberlain
- d. Tom Seaver

29) At what Greenwhich Village corner can you find Dr. Strange's Sanctum Sanctorum?

30) What is Super Chicken's real name?

31) Who was the Herculoids' leader?

32) On what date was Skeezix left on Walt Wallet's doorstep?

33) Who is the catcher on Charlie Brown's baseball team?

34) In what country was *Batman and the Outsiders* formed?

35) Name Tom Slick's race car from the cartoon series.

36) Sam Wilson, the Falcon, started life as a criminal. True or False?

37) Name the two youngsters saved by the animated Moby Dick.

. . . *Answers*

28. a

29. Bleeker Street and Fenno Place

30. Henry Cabot Henhouse III

31. King Zandor

32. February 14, 1921

33. Schroeder

34. Markovia

35. Thunderbolt Grease Slapper

36. False

37. Tom and Tuby

38) Mike Doonesbury's brother is named:
   a. Willy
   b. Thomas
   c. Benjy
   d. Doug

39) Galactus has had seven beings as his heralds. Name them.

40) How did Thor become the Mighty Mightor?

41) From the cartoon series, what is Super President's real name?

42) Name Dick Tracy's two children.

43) What is Elektra's chosen weapon from the comics?

44) Name the cartoon genie conjured by the magic ring shared by Nancy and Chuck.

45) Simple J. Malarkey was Pogo's answer to Senator Joseph McCarthy. True or False?

46) Which of Spider-Man's amazing friends was created for the animated series?

47) What planet is the home of the Guardians of the Galaxy?

48) In *Rocky and Bullwinkle*, what is Rocky's full name?

. . . *Answers*

38. c

39. Silver Surfer, Air Walker I, Air Walker II, Firelord, Destroyer, Terrax, Nova

40. He slammed his club to the ground, calling on the magic within

41. James Norcross

42. Bonnie Braids and Joseph Flintheart

43. A sai

44. Shazzan

45. True

46. Firestar

47. Oa

48. Rocket J. Squirrel

49) While Bugs Bunny never had kids, Sylvester the cat had a son. What was his name?

50) Selina Kyle is better known in comic books as:
   a. The Catwoman
   b. The Harlequin
   c. The Black Canary
   d. The Huntress

51) Name four cartoon series from the Fleisher Studios.

52) Wonder Woman was fashioned from clay. True or False?

53) What did Ignatz Mouse throw in his comic strips and cartoons?

54) In *Mickey's Christmas Carol*, which Disney characters played the Christmas spirits?

55) When Daffy Duck became Duck Dogers, who played his admiring assistant?

56) Jeff MacNelly is famous for two things. What are they?

57) What is Jimmy Olsen's full name?

58) Who was the Great Kazoo's voice from the Flintstones?

. . . *Answers*

49. Junior

50. a

51. *Koko the Clown*, *Betty Boop*, *Popeye*, and *Superman*

52. True

53. Bricks

54. Jiminy Cricket (Past), Willie the Giant (Present), Peg-Leg Pete (Future)

55. Porky Pig

56. Winning two Pulitzer Prizes for editorial cartoons and doing the *Shoe* comic strip

57. James Bartholomew Olsen

58. Comedian Harvey Corman

59) What other Hanna-Barbera creations has Space Ghost adventured with?

60) Name Mickey Mouse's first appearance.

61) Who was Krypton's most accomplished astronaut?

62) Which super-villain is Ka-Zar's brother in the Marvel comics?

63) How did Peabody and Sherman travel through time?

64) Can you name network TV's first prime time cartoon series?

65) Did cartoondom's Gerald McBoing-Boing talk?

66) What was Alvin and the Chipmunks' profession?

67) What did Underdog's girl friend, Sweet Polly Purebread, do for a living?

68) Who is Luke Cage's partner in crime fighting?

69) Which member of the Micronauts spent 1000 years traveling the Microverse in the Marvel comics?

70) Dudley Do-Right had a horse named _____.

71) In the *Speed Racer* cartoons, what was Racer X's name and relationship to Speed?

. . . Answers

59. The Herculoids

60. *Steamboat Willie*, 1928

61. Lara, Superman's mother

62. The Plunderer

63. Via the Wayback Machine

64. *CBS Cartoon Theater* with host Dick Van Dyck

65. No, he made noises sounding like "boing"

66. They were singers

67. She was a newscaster

68. Iron Fist

69. Arcturus Rann

70. Horse

71. Rex, and he was Speed Racer's older brother

72) Who usurped Lillandra's Shi'Ar Empire throne?

73) When Amethyst is on Earth, what are her name and age according to the comic book?

74) Who were the last three people admitted to the Justice League of America?

75) Who comprised the now-defunct comic book team known as the Champions?

76) Can you name Secret Squirrel's accomplice?

77) Name all six types of Kryptonite.

78) In Beetle Bailey, Lieutenant Fuzz's first name is:
   a. Billy
   b. Steve
   c. Sonny
   d. Roger

79) Where did Barry Allen come up with the name "the Flash"?

80) Who created Spider-Man?

81) Who ruled Atlantis 500 years before the time of Conan?

82) What *Laugh-In* regular gave Space Ghost a voice?

. . . *Answers*

72. Deathbird

73. Amy Winston, age 13

74. Gypsy, Vibe, and Commander Steel

75. The Angel and the Ice Man

76. Morocco Mole

77. White, Gold, Blue, Green, Red, and Jewel

78. c

79. Being a comic book collector, he was inspired by the 1940's Flash

80. Stan Lee and Steve Ditko

81. King Kull

82. Gary Owens

83) By whom was Tony Stark, a.k.a. Iron Man, chauffeured around town?

84) Name the brother and sister team in Marvel's *Alpha Flight*.

85) What Egyptian god inspired Marc Spector to become Moon Knight?

86) Who coveted King Leonardo's throne in the cartoon series?

87) The Phantom Stranger's real name and origin have never been revealed in comic books. True or False?

88) Who was known as the Time Master in comic books?
   a. Rip Hunter
   b. Rip Kirby
   c. Rip Cord
   d. Rip Tide

89) Who designed and built the Metal Men in DC comics?

90) Tom and Jerry got to dance with which real hoofer in a movie?

91) Race Bannon, Hadji, and Bandit joined whom on worldwide adventures?

. . . Answers

83. Originally by Happy Hogan and later by James Rhodes

84. Northstar and Aurora

85. Khonshu

86. His villainous brother, Itchy Brother

87. True

88. a

89. Dr. Will Magnus

90. Gene Kelly

91. Johnny Quest

92) Who is the most illustrious inmate at Gotham City's Arkham Asylum?

93) Before Bugs Bunny, Warner Bros. had another cartoon star. Who was he?

94) Whom did Cosmo G. Spacely employ in the cartoons?

95) To which company is Beetle Bailey assigned?

96) When danger appeared, Quick Draw McGraw became which super-hero?

97) Did Barney and Betty Rubble ever have a child of their own?

98) What is Smokey Stover's job?

99) Who turned down Peter Parker's proposal of marriage?
    a. Gwen Stacy
    b. Mary Jane Watson
    c. Felicia Hardy
    d. Betty Brant

100) Where do Rocky and Bullwinkle play football?

101) When the Fantastic Four travel, they take one of two devices. Name them.

. . . *Answers*

92. The Joker

93. Bosko

94. George Jetson

95. A Company

96. El Kabong

97. No, but they adopted Bamm-Bamm

98. He's a fireman

99. b

100. What'samatta U

101. The Pogo Plane and the Fantasticar

102) Who is known as the Hog of Steel?

103) Name the Jetson's robot maid.

104) What kind of animal is Pogo?

105) Where is Professor X's School for Gifted Youngsters located?

106) Name Crusader Rabbit's companion.

107) What does Schroeder want to be?

108) Name Wonder Woman's boyfriend.

109) Where does Billy Batson work?

110) What is Dennis the Menace's last name?

111) In what city does Fat Albert live?

112) Name four comic strips about pilots.

113) Swamp Thing is a transmuted Alec Holland. True or False.

114) *On Stage* featured the life of what actress?

115) Name Hercules's centaur sidekick.

116) Peter Parker takes photos for the *Daily Flash*. True or False.

... *Answers*

102. Wonder Wart-Hog

103. Rosie

104. An opossum

105. Westchester, New York

106. Ragland T. Tiger, a.k.a. Rags

107. A concert pianist

108. Steve Trevor

109. WHIZ, radio and TV

110. Mitchell

111. Philadelphia

112. *Scorchy Smith*, *Buz Sawyer*, *Steve Canyon*, *Johnny Hazard*

113. False

114. Mary Perkins

115. Newton

116. False, he takes photos for the *Daily Bugle*

117) What happened to Moon Maiden?

118) The man who created Courageous Cat and Minute Mouse also created:
   a. Batman
   b. Captain Marvel
   c. Archie
   d. Hawkman

119) Where do the Inhumans currently reside?

120) Name Alvin's brothers.

121) What was the original strip name for *Steve Roper*?

122) Other than Thor, who is the only person worthy enough to wield Mjolnir?

123) Which band did not play at *Bloom County's* US Festival?
   a. The Police
   b. Van Halen
   c. Tess Turbo and the Blackheads
   d. Blue Oyster Cult

124) Other than Wilma, who was in love with Buck Rogers?

125) An alien creature in a funny hat has opposed both Bugs Bunny and Daffy Duck. Where is he from?

. . . *Answers*

117. She died in a booby-trapped car intended for Dick Tracy

118. a

119. The Moon

120. Simon and Theodore

121. Chief Wahoo

122. Beta Ray Bill

123. d

124. Princess Ardala

125. Mars

126) Hanna-Barbera rose to fame by creating what duo for MGM?

127) Name the Marvel team loosely based on DC's Justice League of America?

128) Joe Palooka was undefeated. True or False?

129) The Professor in *Felix the Cat* had a nephew. What was his name?

130) In the cartoons, Mary Jane used what magic words to become Sniffles's size?

131) Apollo 10's capsule and lunar module were named after a pair of comic strip characters. Who were they?

132) Which planet does Charlie-27, a Guardian of the Galaxy, hail from?

133) How tall was the animated King Kong?
    a. 20 feet
    b. 30 feet
    c. 60 feet
    d. 75 feet

134) Name the original strip name for the *Family Circus*.

135) What is the full name of Colossus of the *X-Men*?

136) On what T.V. show could Tom Terrific be found?

... *Answers*

126. Tom and Jerry

127. The Squadron Supreme

128. True

129. Poindexter

130. "Poof Poof Piffles"

131. Charlie Brown was the command module and Snoopy was the lunar module

132. Jupiter

133. c

134. *The Family Circle*

135. Piotr Nikolaievich Rasputin

136. Captain Kangaroo

137) Who did Black Bolt, leader of the Inhumans, marry?

138) What interesting method was used to run the credits in the early *Popeye* cartoons?

139) Who was Rick O'Shay's girl friend, later his wife?

140) Who was Rip Kirby's manservant/best friend?

141) On which floor of the *Daily Bugle* building is the city room?

142) The Fleishers produced how many *Superman* cartoons?
    a. 17
    b. 15
    c. 30
    d. 24

143) Name Mr. Dithers' wife in *Blondie*.

144) Who edits the *Treetops Tattler Tribune* in the comic strips?

145) Which member of the New Mutants has been haunted by a murderous mystical bear?

146) Who was Matthew Murdock's first great love in the Marvel comics?

. . . Answers

137. Medusa

138. The slamming doors of the wooden ship

139. Gaye Abandon

140. Desmond

141. 17th Floor

142. a

143. Cora

144. Mr. Shoemaker

145. Danielle Moonstar

146. Elektra

147) What is Steve Rogers's profession when he's not Captain America?

148) Name the first cartoon to feature Woody Woodpecker.

149) Who created Slam Bradley, Dr. Occult, and Superman?

150) Name the country ruled by Dr. Doom in the Marvel comics.

151) What is Flo Capp's one outside interest?
    a. Gin Rummy
    b. Darts
    c. Bingo
    d. Movies.

152) In the *Spider-Man* comics, who is Felicia Hardy?

153) What is the last name of the family featured in *For Better or For Worse*?

154) Which Marx Brother is the model for Cerebus the Aardvark's adversary, Lord Julius?

155) What do the Guardian, Wildcat, and Atom have in common?

156) Who was Ricochet Rabbit's partner in crime fighting in the cartoons?

. . . Answers

147. He's a commercial artist

148. "Knock Knock"

149. Jerry Seigel and Joe Shuster

150. Latveria

151. c

152. The Black Cat

153. Patterson

154. Groucho

155. They were all trained by the same man

156. Droop-a-long

157) Who tends Dr. Strange's home in the Marvel comics?

158) What super-hero played father figure to the Newsboy Legion?

159) Did Beetle Bailey enlist or was he drafted?

160) Who was the Flash's first opponent when he appeared in 1956?

161) What comic book World War I pilot is known as the Hammer of Hell?

162) Hawk and the Dove, of comic book fame, are cousins. True or False?

163) When Hyram the Fly put on his super-powered glasses, what cartoon hero did he become?

164) What is the name of Lois Lane's sister?

165) Who was Secret Squirrel's dangerous adversary?

166) In comic books, Merlin conjured a demon who lives today. Name him.

167) Who was Clark Kent's childhood sweetheart?

168) Who is Snoopy's arch-enemy?

. . . Answers

157. Wong

158. The Guardian

159. He enlisted

160. The Turtle

161. Hans Von Hammer, Enemy Ace

162. False, they are brothers

163. The Fearless Fly

164. Lucy

165. The Yellow Pinky

166. Etrigan

167. Lana Lang

168. The Red Baron

169) Where do the Super Friends operate?

170) Give Dr. Sivana's full name.

171) What is Fat Freddy's cat named?

172) Buz Sawyer enlisted in which branch of the service?

173) Who was the animated Hercules' most frequent foe?

174) Name Momma's three children.

175) The first herald for the world-eating Galactus was:
   a. Terrax
   b. Nova
   c. Gabriel
   d. Silver Surfer

176) Who raised Peter Parker?

177) The Watcher has a name. What is it?

178) Who was Casper the Friendly Ghost's naughty cousin?

179) Who is Sally Brown's sweet baboo?

180) How long does a charge last in Green Lantern's ring?

. . . Answers

169. The Hall of Justice

170. Thaddeus Bodag Sivana

171. Fat Freddy's Cat

172. Navy Air Force

173. Daedalus

174. Mary Lou, Thomas, and Francis

175. d

176. Aunt May and Uncle Ben

177. Oatu

178. Spooky

179. Linus Van Pelt

180. 24 hours

181) Name Betty Boop's dog.

182) Secret Agent X-9 later became Secret Agent
_____.

183) Where does George Jetson work?

184) The land where Travis Morgan, the Warlord, lives
is called:
   a. Poseidanis
   b. Skataris
   c. Pellucidar
   d. The Savage Land

185) Which super-heroine was a one-time Congress-
woman?

186) Name the *Smilin' Jack* character whose face we
never saw.

187) In *Dick Tracy*, who was Shakey's step-daughter?

188) Scooby Doo is a fearless pet. True or False?

189) Why was Astro Boy built?

190) Who was Reed Richards's first choice for a college
roommate?

191) How is the Sub-Mariner related to Namorita?

... *Answers*

181. Bimbo

182. Corrigan

183. Spacely Space Sprockets

184. b

185. Batgirl

186. Downwind

187. Breathless Mahoney

188. False

189. He was modeled after the scientist's son who was killed in an auto-accident

190. Victor Von Doom

191. First cousin, once removed

192) Name Johnny Q's last name from the *On Stage* strip.

193) What is Project Pegasus in Marvel comics?

194) Who gave voice to Superman in the 1940's and 1960's cartoons?

195) Who is Steve Roper's best friend?

196) What book did Dr. Strange use to rid Earth of vampires?

197) Which two *Doonesbury* characters went off in search of America?

198) Which comic strip was never turned into a Broadway musical?
    a. Li'l Abner
    b. Annie
    c. Pogo
    d. Peanuts

199) Who was the physical model for the devil in *Fantasia's* Night on Bald Mountain?

200) Ras al Ghul has a daughter devoted to Batman. Name her.

201) Wilson Fisk is better known as Marvel's Kingpin. True or False?

... *Answers*

192. Quandraxmus

193. A government installation to contain and study super-powered criminals

194. Bud Collier

195. Mike Nomad

196. *The Darkhold*

197. Mike Doonesbury and Mark Slackmeyer

198. c

199. Bela Lugosi

200. Talia

201. True

202) Felix the Cat always ended his show with a phrase. What was it?

203) Where did Mighty Mouse get his super-powers?

204) Marvel's Red Wolf is a member of which Indian tribe?
- a. Hakowie
- b. Cheyenne
- c. Blackfoot
- d. Apache

205) What is Buck Rogers's real first name?

206) What was the worst thing to happen to Yaz Pistachio on her prom night in *Bloom County*?

207) In Marvel comics, Pangea was originally designed to perform what function?

208) Name the Colonel who always tried to remove the Go-Go Gophers in the cartoon series.

209) The Catwoman has gone straight. True or False.

210) Arak's friend Valda has a nickname in the DC comics. What is it?

211) Which comic book robotic heroes were based on elements?

. . . Answers

202. "Rightie-o!"

203. The Supermarket

204. b

205. Anthony

206. Steve Dallas was so drunk, he threw up on her during the spotlight dance

207. It was built by the ancient Atlanteans to be an "amusement park"

208. Kit Coyote

209. True

210. The Iron Maiden

211. The Metal Men

212) Which comic strip was banned from *Stars and Stripes*?
  a. Beetle Bailey
  b. Peanuts
  c. Popeye
  d. Doonesbury

213) Who is Wonder Woman's mother?

214) Milton the Monster was built by which duo in the cartoon series?

215) What is the name of General Halftrack's wife in Beetle Bailey?

216) What was Secret Squirrel's code number in the cartoon series?

217) Who was trying to rule the Microverse in the *Micronauts* comic book?

218) Peter Canon has trained himself to near perfection and is better known by which super-hero name?

219) Which comic book great provided the art direction for the *Space Ghost* cartoon series?

220) What is the name of the *Family Circus's* dog?

221) Who delivers the *Treetops Tattler Tribune* in *Shoe*?

. . . Answers

212. a

213. Queen Hyppolita

214. Professor Weirdo and Count Kook

215. Martha

216. OOO

217. Baron Karza

218. Thunderbolt

219. Alex Toth

220. Barfy

221. Loon

222) For how long could Negative Man stay outside Larry Trainor's body?

223) Which space sector is patrolled by the Green Lantern of Earth in the DC comics?

224) Where did Matt Murdock get the name Daredevil?

225) Who is the Cimmerian destined to be a king?

226) Which comic strip has Mort Walker not been associated with?
   a. *Boner's Ark*
   b. *Tank McNamara*
   c. *Beetle Bailey*
   d. *Hi and Lois*

227) UNICEF named which cartoon mouse its official ambassador in 1961 and 1962?

228) Name four members of the illustrious Oyl family from comic strip fame.

229) Which mutant heroine just wants to be left alone to become a rock star?

230) Name the comic book that started as a spoof of barbarians before taking on a life of its own.

231) Who owns the Daily Planet?

. . . Answers

222. 60 seconds

223. 2814

224. In his youth, he was called Daredevil by taunting peers

225. Conan

226. b

227. Mighty Mouse

228. Olive, Castor, Nana, and Cole

229. Dazzler

230. Cerebus the Aardvark

231. Galaxy Broadcasting Corporation

QUESTIONS

232) Who was Dick Dastardly's pet?
   a. Blubber
   b. Rufus
   c. Slag
   d. Muttley

233) Whom did Nell love more, Dudley Do-Right or his horse?

234) What was the radio station Doonesbury's Mark Slackmeyer worked on?

235) Which super-villain inadvertently brought about the birth of Batgirl?

236) The Elongated Man keeps his identity obscured. True or False?

237) What was Buck Rogers's companion Wilma's last name?

238) In *Bloom County*, what is young Binkley's first name?

239) Who is Rocky's and Bullwinkle's ever-lost friend?

240) Name the two tunes used in *Looney Tunes* and *Merry Melodies*.

241) Who defied government orders and commanded a spaceship into unpredictable cosmic rays?

49

. . . *Answers*

232. d

233. Horse

234. WBBY

235. Killer Moth

236. False

237. Deering

238. Michael

239. Wrongway Peachfuzz

240. "Merry-Go-Round Broken Down" and "Merrily We Roll Along"

241. Reed Richards

242) Who first gave voice to Woody Woodpecker?
   a. Lucille Bliss
   b. Don Messick
   c. Mrs. Walter Lantz
   d. Mel Blanc

243) In the comic strip what does Botley do?

244) What does the "B.O." stand for in B.O. Plenty?

245) What was the first full-length cartoon?

246) In the Marvel stories, who was Dracula's hated daughter?

247) What has retarded Nick Fury's aging in the Marvel comics?

248) There was never a cartoon series based on Dr. Doolittle. True or False?

249) Which member of *Charlie's Angels* sang vocals for Josie and the Pussycats?

250) Irwin the Troll, in *Broom Hilda*, has a nephew. Name him.

251) Name the two mystical ravens Odin has at his command.

252) What profession does Steve Roper practice?

. . . *Answers*

242. d

243. Construction worker for the Drudge Corporation

244. Bob Oscar

245. Snow White and the Seven Dwarves

246. Lilith

247. The Infinity Formula

248. False

249. Cheryl Ladd

250. Nerwin

251. Hugin and Munin

252. Newspaper Editor

253) Name Rick O'Shay's gunslinging best friend.

254) What animals did The Amazing Three masquerade as?

255) Name the *On Stage* character whose face was never seen.

256) Name the members of *Batman's* Outsiders.

257) Name Dennis the Menace's next door neighbors.

258) T'Challa, the Black Panther, is king of what hidden African nation?

259) What is Boris Badenov's companion's name?

260) Rerun is Charlie Brown's little brother. True or False.

261) Who is the Incredible Hulk in reality?

262) Name Courageous Cat's partner.

263) What "magic" does Mandrake employ?

264) The original Human Torch was a man bathed in chemicals. True or False.

265) Who ran the pet store where McGilla Gorilla lived?

. . . Answers

253. Hipshot Percussion

254. A rabbit, a horse and a duck

255. Maximus

256. Katana, Halo, Geo-Force, Metamorpho, and Black Lightning

257. George and Martha Wilson

258. Wakanda

259. Natasha

260. False, Rerun is Lucy and Linus's little brother

261. Dr. Robert Bruce Banner

262. Minute Mouse

263. Hypnotism

264. False, he was an android

265. Mr. Peeples

266) To gain extra strength, what did the animated Hercules do?

267) Who was Speed Racer's younger brother?

268) Who was Joe Palooka's best friend?

269) Who was the first X-Man to die in battle?

270) After five hundred years of life, what happened to the Ancient One?

271) Why did Li'l Abner marry Daisy Mae?

272) Which couple started out as children on one cartoon series and had grown-up adventures in another?

273) Boris and Natasha were always after a hat. Name the hat.

274) Name the President at *Doonesbury's* college.

275) Harriet, the only female bird in Snoopy's camping ground, excels at something. What?

276) Who is Scooby Doo's son?

277) Which of the following is not a real super-hero:
    a. Captain Atom
    b. Captain Power
    c. Captain Universe
    d. Captain Savage

. . . Answers

266. He put on his magic ring

267. Spridle

268. "Gentle Giant," Humphrey Pennyworth

269. Thunderbird

270. He became "one" with the Universe

271. He swore by Fearless Fosdick's actions, and when the detective married, Abner had no choice

272. Pebbles and Bamm-Bamm

273. Kerwood Derby

274. King

275. Angel food cake with seven-minute frosting

276. Scrappy Doo

277. b

278) Name the three locations of the Justice League of America's headquarters.

279) How did *Bloom County's* Cutter John get to meet Bobbi Harlow?

280) Thor's ladylove, Sif, has a brother named Heimdall. True or False?

281) Name the Hot Wheel Club's two major competing clubs.

282) Who designed the look for the Pink Panther?

283) *Little Iodine* was a spin-off from which comic strip?

284) Name the various costumed personas of Dr. Henry Pym.

285) What is the greatest source of "white" magic in the Marvel Universe?

286) Who is Daddy Warbucks's unrequited love?

287) Who was Nell's father in *Dudley Do-Right*?

288) Which century did Buck Rogers wake up in?

289) Mera, former Queen of a water dimension, married which DC super-hero?

... *Answers*

278. A mountain, a space satellite, and a rebuilt factory in Detroit

279. His wheelchair was out of control and he literally swept Bobbi off her feet

280. True

281. Stuff Haley and his Bombers and Dexter Carter and his Demons

282. Friz Freleng

283. *There Ought to be a Law*

284. Ant Man, Giant Man, Goliath, and Yellowjacket

285. The Book of the Vashanti

286. Angela Pease

287. Inspector Fenwick

288. 25th Century

289. Aquaman

QUESTIONS

290) Former teacher Jonathan Crane is also one of Batman's deadliest foes. Who is he?

291) How many people have been Captain America?

292) Who built Frankenstein Jr. in the cartoon series?

293) Who rules the Inhumans?

294) Commissioner Dolan's daughter, who loves the Spirit, is named:
   a. Joan
   b. Catherine
   c. Ellen
   d. Nancy

295) In *Bloom County*, who is always awakened by his son with the latest gossip?

296) Which comic strip character is Beetle Bailey's sister?

297) Who joined the Legion of Super-Heroes first, Superboy or Supergirl?

298) Where does Barry Allen keep his Flash costume?

299) Who was Tom of THUMB's partner?

. . . *Answers*

290. The Scarecrow

291. Four: Steve Rogers, Spirit of '76, Patriot, and a man who changed his name to Steve Rogers

292. A boy genius named Buzz

293. Black Bolt

294. c

295. Tom Binkley

296. Lois of *Hi and Lois*

297. Superboy

298. Compressed in his ring

299. Swinging Jack

300) In *For Better or For Worse*, Uncle Phil plays:
   a. Trombone
   b. Trumpet
   c. Tuba
   d. Saxophone

301) Where does Wonder Woman hail from?

302) Who is Superman's mermaid friend?

303) Jan and Jace aided which intergalactic cartoon hero?

304) In how many animated cartoons has Uncle Scrooge McDuck appeared?

305) Where did Peter Parker go to college?

306) Which New Mutant has a brother in the *X-Men*?

307) Who was the Sub-Mariner's mother?

308) Amos T. Halftrack runs what base in the comic strips?

309) The name of the newspaper in *Shoe* is the *Treetops Tattler Tribune*. True or False?

310) Who is the woman loved by the Silver Surfer?

311) Who led the elves before Cutter in *Elfquest*?

. . . Answers

300. b

301. Paradise Island

302. Lori Lemaris

303. Space Ghost

304. Two

305. Empire State University

306. Ilyana Rasputin

307. Princess Fenn

308. Camp Swampy

309. True

310. Shalla Bal

311. Bearclaw

312) What was unique about the *Winky Dink* animated series?

313) What can be found, in addition to Man-Thing, in Man-Thing's swamp?

314) Who raised Scott Free on Apokolips before he escaped to Earth?

315) Which *Bloom County* resident wreaks havoc with a computer?

316) Darkseid's avenging son is
    a. Lightray
    b. Metron
    c. Desaad
    d. Orion

317) Name the Blackhawks.

318) Prince Valiant was prince of what?

319) Name Batman's butler Alfred's daughter.

320) Where did Fred Flintstone work?

321) What was Joe Palooka's profession?

322) Name the leader of DC Comics' Omega Men.

323) What's Daffy Duck's usual closing line?

... Answers

312. You could buy a plastic screen to draw Winky Dink out of danger

313. The Nexus of All Realities

314. Granny Goodness

315. Oliver Wendell Jones

316. d

317. Chop-Chop, Stan, Andre, Olaf, Hendrickson, and Chuck

318. The country Thule

319. Julia

320. Rock Head and Quarry Care Construction Co.

321. Boxer

322. Primus

323. "You're despicable!"

324) Who is Master of the Mystic Arts?

325) Name both men to assume the identity of Ant Man.

326) Name Matt Murdock's law partner.

327) What did Mighty Mouse always sing as he went into action?

328) Where does the Spirit maintain his headquarters?

329) Skyler, in *Shoe*, is a failure at which sport:
   a. Volleyball
   b. Soccer
   c. Basketball
   d. Wrestling

330) What is the connection between Hulk and She-Hulk?

331) Name the pirate with whom Conan had a three year affair.

332) Porky Pig had a girl friend. Name her.

333) What is the relationship between Superman and Supergirl?

334) What does Steve Dallas do for a living?

. . . *Answers*

324. Dr. Strange

325. Henry Pym and Scott Lang

326. Foggy Nelson

327. "Here I come to save the day!"

328. Underneath Wildwood Cemetery

329. c

330. First cousins

331. Belit

332. Petunia

333. Cousins

334. Lawyer

335) Who is the most beloved figure in DC Comics' *Gemworld*?

336) Who put together the current incarnation of the Defenders?

337) Casper the Friendly Ghost frolicked with which witch?

338) Who won the Instrumentality-Monarchy war despite Dreadstar's help in the comic book series?

339) Bugs always finds himself at the wrong end of a gun, usually toted by which two men?

340) Who make up Marvel Comics' *Nightwing Restorations*?

341) Who invented the Phantom Zone projector?

342) Where was Mr. Peeples' Pet Shop located?

343) What shape-shifting menace did Rom come to Earth to fight?

344) After leading the Howling Commandos, what did Nick Fury go on to lead?

345) Who leads the band of elves in *Elfquest*?

346) Within the strip, has any *Doonesbury* character appeared on the cover of a real-life national magazine?

. . . *Answers*

335. Amethyst

336. The Beast

337. Wendy the Good Witch

338. The Church of Instrumentality

339. Yosemite Sam and Elmer Fudd

340. Misty Knight and Colleen Wing

341. Jor-El

342. Los Angeles

343. The Dire Wraiths

344. SHIELD

345. Cutter

346. Yes, *Time*

347) Felix the Cat had a nemesis named The Professor. True or False?

348) In addition to the cloak of levitation, what does Dr. Strange always have with him?

349) Who was the second person ever to wear Iron Man's armor?

350) Name Bugs Bunny's girl friend.

351) Garfield's owner, John, is continually asking out one particular woman. What is her profession?

352) Who provided the technology giving the Falcon his mini-jet wings?

353) What spotted creature did Beany and Cecil chase in the cartoons?

354) Which *Peanuts* character has naturally curly hair?

355) When Mighty Mouse was conceived, what was his original name?

356) Who were the first graduates of the Legion of Super-Heroes Academy?

357) In their early adventures, what alien planet did Ruff and Reddy go to?

. . . Answers

347. True

348. The Eye of Agamotto

349. Happy Hogan

350. Daisy

351. She's Garfield's veterinarian

352. The Black Panther (from Wakanda)

353. Tearalong, the Dotted Lion

354. Frieda

355. Supermouse

356. Timber Wolf and Chemical King

357. Munimula

358) Name Daisy the dog's owner.
    a. Hi and Lois
    b. Dagwood and Blondie
    c. Ellie and Steve
    d. Dick and Tess

359) Superman keeps his street clothes compressed in a belt buckle. True or False?

360) In what year did Peanuts and Beetle Bailey first appear?

361) In her cartoons, did Betty Boop ever go topless?

362) Which cartoon series used human lips to make the show look real?

363) Name Moose Mason's girl friend.

364) Where is the Outsider's headquarters, from the DC comics series?

365) Gunner, Sarge, Capt. Johnny Cloud, and Captain Storm have what in common?

366) Pogo first appeared in:
    a. Cartoon
    b. Comic strip
    c. Comic book
    d. Novel

... *Answers*

358. b

359. False, they're kept in a cape pouch

360. 1950

361. Yes, often

362. *Space Angel* and *Clutch Cargo*

363. Midge

364. The secondary Batcave, beneath the Wayne Foundation building

365. They are the Losers, a WW II suicide squad

366. c

QUESTIONS

367) Did Li'l Abner's Fearless Fosdick ever have his own TV series?

368) Who was Tom Terrific's frequent nemesis?

369) Who was Joe Palooka's manager?

370) The Shining Knight, of comic books, is named Sir Gerrold. True or False?

371) Who was the original voice of Mickey Mouse?

372) The X-Men had an FBI contact initially. Name him.

373) Who was George of the Jungle a friend of?

374) Buck Rogers's greatest opponent was:
   a. Killer Kane
   b. Dr. Doom
   c. Drax
   d. Dark Destroyer

375) Who was the first Justice League of America member to resign for a length of time?

376) What is the connection between New Krypton and Daxam?

377) Who is Tobor?

. . . Answers

367. Yes, briefly in the early 1950's

368. Crabby Appleton

369. Knobby Walsh

370. False, he's Sir Justin

371. Creator Walt Disney

372. Fred Duncan

373. You and me

374. a

375. Wonder Woman

376. After its establishment, the people changed the name sometime before the 30th Century

377. The Eighth Man

378) Who was the Lone Ranger's crimefighting great nephew?

379) Which Dogpatch inhabitant always had a cloud over his head?

380) Where are Rocket J. Squirrel and Bullwinkle from?

381) What are the given names for the heroes best known as Aqualad and Aquagirl?

382) Who framed Yellowjacket, forcing him out of the Avengers?

383) Name the inventor in Daddy Warbucks's employ.

384) To operate underwater, which animated hero chewed Aqua Gum?

385) What is Super Chicken's partner's name?

386) Flash Gordon most often battled evil on which exotic planet?

387) Why is sheepherder Marcus known as the Golden Gladiator in comic books?

388) Captain America's first partner, Bucky, had a real name. What was it?

. . . Answers

378. The Green Hornet

379. Joe Bskfskt

380. Frostbite Falls

381. Garth and Tula

382. Egghead

383. Professor Eon

384. Marine Boy

385. Fred

386. Mongo

387. The Praetor granted Marcus a solid-gold helmet, signifying he was best gladiator in all of Ancient Rome

388. James Buchanan Barnes

389) What was the original name Charles Schulz had for *Peanuts*?

390) Name cartoondom's two Moon Men.

391) Give the full name for *Terry and the Pirates'* Connie?

392) Freedom's Five was Marvel's super-hero team during which world war?

393) Dudley Do-Right's girlfriend Nell's last name is:
   a. Jones
   b. Smith
   c. Simon
   d. Fenwick

394) How is Abigail Arcane related to the villainous opponent of the Swamp Thing, Anton Arcane?

395) *Bloom County's* Steve Dallas appeared in a rock video with which band?

396) Which *Doonesbury* character was likely to turn into a werewolf?

397) How did Captain America survive World War II to still be 30 years old today?

398) Name Penelope Pitstop's wacky race car.

. . . Answers

389. *Li'l Folks*

390. Ridney and Cloyde

391. George Webster Confucious

392. World War I

393. d

394. She is his niece

395. Tess Turbo and the Blackheads

396. Bernie

397. He was frozen in a block of ice for years

398. The Compact Pussycat

399) The *Hardy Boys* cartoon series featured them traveling the world as:
   a. Pingpong players
   b. Students
   c. Singers
   d. Tourists

400) Who bestowed great power upon Captain Britain?

401) Name Hagar the Horrible's dog.

402) Who is OMAC's grandson?

403) Sarge Steel's secretary's name is Velda. True or False?

404) What element was added when Archie and friends were brought to TV?

405) When a person receives the Uni-Power, who does he become?

406) Did we ever learn the first name of Joanie Caucus's first husband?

407) Which member of the Green Lantern corps failed to prevent Krypton from blowing up?

408) Heckle and Jeckle have differing backgrounds. Which is from Brooklyn and which from England?

. . . Answers

399. c

400. Merlin the magician and the Goddess of the Northern Skies

401. Snert

402. Kamandi, the Last Boy on Earth

403. False, it's Bess

404. They were made into a rock band

405. Captain Universe

406. Yes, Clint

407. Tomar-Re

408. Heckle hails from Brooklyn while Jeckle is from England

409) *On Stage's* Mary Perkins is both a successful actress and wife. What is her husband's name?

410) Eve Eden is secretly:
   a. Nightshade
   b. Nightwing
   c. Nighthawk
   d. Nightowl

411) Name Conchy's cave-dwelling friends.

412) Name the various super-teams to which the Angel has belonged.

413) Who was the criminal known as the Black Knight?

414) Shep was the name of George of the Jungle's pet elephant. True or False?

415) Who was Dick Tracy's second partner?

416) Binkley has his hormones carbonated by whom in *Bloom County*?

417) Who has always given the gang at Walden Puddle spiritual advice?

418) Name the Oan to unleash evil in the DC Universe.

. . . *Answers*

409. Photographer Pete Fletcher

410. a

411. Patch and Duff

412. The X-Men, the Champions, and the Defenders

413. Nathan Garrett

414. True

415. Sam Ketcham

416. Blondie, the new girl from LA

417. Rev. Scott Sloan

418. Krona

419) The fearsome Blastaar comes from:
   a. the Phantom Zone
   b. the Survival Zone
   c. the Negative Zone
   d. Zone of Darkness

420) How did Super President gain his powers on the animated series?

421) What was unique about the cartoon character Spy Shadow?

422) Name the thing that turned weakling Steve Rogers into Captain America.

423) While riding across country Doonesbury met and invited Rick Redfern to visit his home. True or False?

424) What does Peppermint Patty always call Charlie Brown?

425) Brother Voodoo is actually two brothers. Name them.

426) What is the name of Dudley Do-Right's horse?

427) Who came first, Captain America or the Original Shield?

428) Which TV series never had its own comic strip:
   a. Dallas   c. Dynasty
   b. Ben Casey   d. Dark Shadows

. . . *Answers*

419. c

420. He was accidentally exposed to unpredictable cosmic rays

421. He was able to operate independently from his shadow

422. The Super Soldier Formula

423. False

424. Chuck

425. Jericho and Daniel Drumm

426. Horse

427. The Original Shield

428. c

429) Who rules the island Conchy lives on in the comic strip?

430) The mutant known as the Blob has a real name. What is it?

431) Which Wacky Racers spun off into their own series?

432) The *Archie Comedy Hour* introduced a new character. Who was she?

433) Who do Herb and Tootsie live next door to?

434) What does Buddy Blank's name, OMAC, stand for?

435) Captain Ulysses Hazard was a World War II operative code-named:
    a. Mockingbird
    b. Sparrow
    c. Snake Eyes
    d. Gravedigger

436) A gentlemanly gangster spent a lot of time with Mary Perkins. Name him.

437) The network cartoon series *The Adventures of Gulliver* was faithful to the novel. True or False?

438) Charles Boyer inspired a cartoon skunk. Who?

. . . Answers

429. Chief

430. Fred J. Dukes

431. Penelope Pitstop and Dick Dastardly

432. Sabrina, the teenage witch

433. Blondie and Dagwood

434. One Man Army Corps

435. d

436. Johnny Q

437. False

438. Pepe Le Pew

439) In which century can you find the Legion of Super-Heroes?

440) What is Blondie's maiden name?

441) Scott Summers's father is a member of the Starjammers. Name him.

442) Who "haunts" the Haunted Tank?

443) Name the apartment complex where the Jetsons reside.

444) Mockingbird is chairman of the West Coast Avengers. True or False.

445) Name the scar-faced bounty hunter of *The Old West*.

446) Ray Palmer, the Atom, is married to lawyer Jean Loring. True or False.

447) Name the child left on a doorstep at the beginning of *Gasoline Alley*.

448) Bobbi Harlow, in *Bloom County*, has two interesting relatives. One is Yaz Pistachio. Name the other.

449) Name the club Jack Wheeler formed on TV's *Hot Wheels*.

450) What kind of dog is Scooby Doo?

. . . Answers

439. 30th

440. Boopadoop

441. Corsair

442. The ghost of General Jeb Stuart

443. Skypad Apartments

444. False, her husband, Hawkeye, is chairman

445. Jonah Hex

446. False, they're divorced

447. Skeezix

448. Quiche Lorraine

449. The Hot Wheel Club

450. A great dane

451) Who are comic books' Champions of Xandar?

452) Which of the following was created by the team of Siegel and Shuster?
   a. Dr. Fate
   b. Dr. Mystic
   c. Dr. Occult
   d. Dr. Druid

453) What was the business of the animated Sky Hawks?

454) Which city-slicker had the power to whammy people in Dogpatch?

455) Scatman Crothers served as the voice of which animated Harlem Globetrotter?

456) Who is the fast-talking politician in *Grin and Bear It*?

457) Deathlok is from an alternate future of the 1990's. True or False?

458) Name the demon that inhabited Johnny Blaze's body in the Marvel comics.

459) Where could the Reluctant Dragon be found?

460) Jack Kirby did a comic strip adaptation of a science fiction film. Name it.

. . . Answers

451. Nova-Prime, Protector, Powerhouse, and Comet

452. c

453. Air transport and emergency rescue

454. Evil-Eye Fleagle

455. Meadowlark Lemon

456. Senator Snort

457. True

458. Zarathos

459. The English village of Willowmarsh

460. *The Black Hole*

461) How many Crimson Dynamos have opposed Iron Man?

462) In which century do the Guardians of the Galaxy operate?

463) Mary Worth had the nickname Apple Mary during the depression. True or False?

464) *Where's Huddles* was an animated summer series about:
    a. Baseball
    b. Soccer
    c. Football
    d. Basketball

465) Sabrina appeared in cartoons with the Groovy Goolies. Who were they?

466) Which came first, in print: *Wizard of Id* or *B.C.*?

467) Which cast member of the *Funky Winkerbean* strip spun off into his own strip?

468) What race threatens Earth's survival in Marvel's *30th Century*?
    a. A-Chiltarians
    b. Brood
    c. Levians
    d. Badoon

... Answers

461. Five

462. 30th Century

463. True

464. c

465. Dracula, Frankenstein, and the Wolfman

466. *B.C.* although *Wizard of Id* was created first

467. John Darling

468. d

469) When Cutter John and the animals play *Star Trek*, Opus is Mr. Sulu. True or False?

470) Which comic strips became animated for *Archie's TV Funnies*?

471) Name the two aides Daddy Warbucks works with.

472) Tess Truheart married which plainclothes detective?

473) Barry Allen was splashed in chemicals and became which super-hero?

474) When Superman needs to get away from it all, where does he go?

475) In the comics, stuntman Dan Cassidy was magically trapped in a demon outfit. What is the name of the outfit?

476) *Beany and Cecil* started out as a cartoon show. True or False?

477) What famous radio duo performed the voices for *Calvin and the Colonel*?

478) How does Alley Oop travel through time?

479) Scott Summers has a brother Alex in the Marvel comics. What is his super-hero name?

. . . Answers

469. False, he's Mr. Spock

470. Dick Tracy, Nancy, Broom Hilda, Captain and the Kids, Moon Mullins, Smokey Stover, The Drop-Outs, and Emmy Lou

471. Punjab and the Asp

472. Dick Tracy

473. The Flash

474. The Fortress of Solitude

475. Blue Devil

476. False, it began as a puppet show

477. Freeman Godson and Charles Correll, a.k.a. Amos 'n' Andy

478. Professor Wonmung's time machine

479. Alex's code name is Havoc

480) Who was the first masked comic strip hero?

481) Rom — Spaceknight — hails from what planet?

482) Name George Jetson's daughter:
   a. Trudy
   b. Suzie
   c. Judy
   d. Janet

483) *Terry and the Pirates* featured the sultry Dragon Lady. What was her real name?

484) What is the name of Barney Google's horse?

485) How was Top Cat known to his cartoon friends?

486) What is Green Lantern's only weakness?

487) The Avengers' mansion can be found where in Manhattan?

488) Which comic strip was not created by Milt Caniff?
   a. *Terry and the Pirates*
   b. *Steve Canyon*
   c. *Rip Kirby*
   d. *Male Cale*

489) Who is Casper the Friendly Ghost's girl friend?

490) Marvel's original Captain Mar-Vell died in what manner?

. . . Answers

480. The Phantom

481. Galador

482. d

483. Lai Choi San

484. Sparkplug

485. T.C.

486. His power ring cannot affect anything yellow

487. Fifth Avenue, by Central Park

488. c

489. Poli

490. He died from cancer

491) Miss Buxley is secretary to what commanding officer?

492) Whom did Friz Freleng add to the Warner Bros. cartoon ranks?

493) What is the mother's name in the *Family Circus*?

494) Jack Kirby's intertwined stories in *New Gods, Mister Miracle, Jimmy Olsen* and the *Forever People* form what saga?

495) Television reporter Jack Ryder can become:
   a. Creeper
   b. Captain Marvel
   c. The Question
   d. Mr. A.

496) Who was the first ruler of the Eternals?

497) Name the device used by the New Gods which has almost-magical properties.

498) Who is stationed at Camp Swampy in the comic strips?

499) Who is Westview High's band director in *Funky Winkerbean*?

500) Who discovered the animated King Kong?

. . . *Answers*

491. General Halftrack in *Beetle Bailey*

492. Porky Pig

493. Thel

494. *The Fourth World*

495. a

496. Zuras

497. Mother Box

498. Beetle Bailey

499. Harry L. Dinkle

500. Professor Bond and his children, Bobby and Susan

501) What type of plant does Broom Hilda sell?

502) Pioneer Winsor McCay gave us one of the first cartoons. What was it?

503) Name the Fabulous Furry Freak Brothers.

504) What are the names of Superman's natural parents?

505) What does Freddy Freeman say to become Captain Marvel Jr.?

506) Who always tried to jail Krazy Kat?

507) Who was Mandrake's associate?

508) What gives the Blue Beetle his powers?

509) Which super-hero had a drinking problem:
   a. The Atom
   b. Green Arrow
   c. Falcon
   d. Iron Man

510) How did Felix the Cat get out of trouble?

511) Who brought Flash Gordon to Mongo for the first time?

512) Who shot Bruce Wayne's parents?

. . . Answers

501. Venus Nose Trap

502. *Gertie the Dinosaur*

503. Fat Freddy, Freewheelin' Frank, and Phineas

504. Jor-El and Lara

505. "Captain Marvel"

506. Offissa B. Pupp

507. Lothar

508. An ancient Egyptian scarab

509. d

510. He reached into his bag of tricks

511. Dr. Hans Zarkov

512. Joe Chill

513) How does Dick Tracy keep in touch with his fellow officers?

514) Name Donald Duck's nephews and Uncle.

515) What does SHIELD stand for?

516) Popeye's chief adversary had two cartoon names. What were they?

517) Lancelot Strong was the second man to become the Shield. True or False?

518) Conchy is a:
    a. Stockbroker
    b. Beachcomber
    c. Chef
    d. Reporter

519) Who runs Andy Capp's favorite pub?

520) Name Marvel's first fan club.

521) Mentor of Titan had two children in the Marvel comics. Name them.

522) Goldie Gold's friend, Action Jack, had a last name and a profession. What were they?

523) Some comic strip storylines have run more than a year. True or False?

. . . *Answers*

513. His two-way wrist radio

514. Huey, Dewey, and Louie—Uncle Scrooge McDuck

515. Supreme Headquarters International Espionage Law-enforcement Division

516. Brutus and Bluto

517. True

518. b

519. Jackie

520. The Merry Marvel Marching Society

521. Eros and Thanos

522. Travis—a journalist

523. True

524) Name Reed and Susan Richards's son.

525) Why must the Inhuman leader Black Bolt never speak?

526) What made the short-lived *Star Hawks* strip so unique?

527) How does Alley Oop learn the language of the various times he visits?

528) John Blackstar was swept into another universe and confronted:
   - a. Overdog
   - b. Overmind
   - c. Overlord
   - d. Overeasy

529) Billie Sol Wrightoff is the broker to which comic strip journalist?

530) Peg-Leg Pete never appeared in the Mickey Mouse comic strip. True or False?

531) What character did Tex Avery first create upon arriving at MGM?

532) What is Dondi's adoptive last name?

533) Which two Inhumans have been a part of the Fantastic Four?

. . . Answers

524. Franklin Benjamin Richards

525. The barest whisper would cause a mountain to shatter

526. It ran twice the size of any normal strip

527. Time travel imparts limited telepathy to Alley Oop

528. c

529. Cosmo Fishhawk

530. False

531. Screwball Squirrel

532. Wills

533. Crystal and Medusa

534) What is the last name of Sugar of *Sugar and Spike*?

535) What does Tank McNamara do for a living?

536) Who is the comic strips' world's richest man?

537) *The Saga of Chip Balloo* was the first name for which scientifically based animated series?

538) Which *Bloom County* characters were lifted from Berke Breathed's first strip, the *Academia Waltz*?

539) The Vision is actually a reconstructed version of the original Human Torch. True or False?

540) To train his students, Professor X developed what unique method?

541) Did we ever hear Mr. Mum speak?

542) What famous magician attended the Phantom's wedding?

543) Which famous jazzman performed opposite Betty Boop in three of her cartoons?

544) What was the first cartoon to feature sound?

545) When not fighting crime, what did Underdog do for a living?

. . . Answers

534. Plumm

535. Sports reporter

536. Oliver "Daddy" Warbucks

537. Jonny Quest

538. Cutter, then Saigon, then John and Steve Dallas

539. True

540. The Danger Room

541. No

542. Mandrake

543. Cab Calloway

544. *Steamboat Willy* in 1928

545. He was Shoeshine, a shoeshine boy

546) Beetle Bailey's buddy, Killer, has a last name:
   a. Thriller
   b. Miller
   c. Diller
   d. Tiller

547) Luke Cage is known by two other names. What are they?

548) Name the Ranger who was always after Yogi Bear.

549) In what mystical land did Iron Fist receive his training?

550) Who were the three partners of Captain America?

551) Who knows?

552) Who created *Captain America*, the *Newsboy Legion*, and *Romance* comics?

553) What was the justification used by Mr. Peabody to adopt Sherman?

554) Who was the Hulk's first friend?

555) Name the dog in the Yankee Doodle cartoons.

556) Who leads Easy Company in the DC comics during World War II?

. . . *Answers*

546. c

547. Powerman and Hero for Hire

548. Ranger Rick

549. K'un Lun

550. Bucky Barnes, the Falcon, and Nomad

551. The Shadow knows

552. Joe Simon and Jack Kirby

553. If a boy could own a dog, a dog could own a boy

554. Rick Jones

555. Chopper

556. Sergeant Rock

557) In *Beany and Cecil*, what is Cecil's full name?

558) What was the name of Speed Racer's car?

559) What was unusual about Alexandra's appearance in Josie and the Pussycats?

560) The Comet is related to what other super-hero from the comic books?

561) In which Woody Woodpecker cartoon was his theme song introduced?

562) What was the space adventure cartoon series to feature Yogi Bear and Huckleberry Hound together?

563) Who were the bulldog father and son seen frequently in the *Tom and Jerry* cartoons?

564) The Nuclear Man is more commonly known in comic books as:
    a. Captain Atom
    b. Nuklon
    c. Firestorm
    d. Reactron

565) In the cartoons, who was Hokie Wolf's sidekick?

566) In Ruff and Reddy, one was a dog, the other a cat. Which was which?

. . . *Answers*

557. Cecil the Sea Sick Sea Serpent

558. The Mach Five

559. She had black hair with a white streak

560. The Hangman, who was his brother

561. *Wet Blanket Coverage*

562. *Yogi's Space Race*

563. Spike and Tyke

564. c

565. Dingaling

566. Ruff was the cat, Reddy the dog

567) Where do Krazy Kat, Ignatz Mouse and Offissa Pupp live?

568) *Winnie Winkle* originally featured her adventurous brother. Name him.

569) What is the name of Thor's enchanted hammer?

570) Where do the Fantastic Four keep their headquarters?

571) In *Rocky and Bullwinkle*, Natasha's last name is:
   a. Smith
   b. Jones
   c. Battinov
   d. Fataly

572) Before Olive Oyl met Popeye she was engaged to someone. Name him.

573) Maggie and Jiggs had a beautiful daughter. What was her name?

574) Who was always called upon to stop Katnip's troublemaking?

575) Name the people who have been Robin the Boy Wonder.

576) Name Canada's super-hero team in the Marvel comics.

. . . Answers

567. Coconino County

568. Perry Winkle

569. Mjolnir

570. The Baxter Building, Manhattan

571. d

572. Ham Gravy

573. Norah

574. Herman the mouse

575. Bruce Wayne, Dick Grayson, Jason Todd

576. Alpha Flight

577) King Leonardo's partner, Odie Colognie, was a tiger in the cartoon. True or False?

578) What were the first names of the Katzenjammer Kids?

579) Name the lodge to which Fred Flintstone and Barney Rubble belonged.

580) What comic strip, within Li'l Abner, was a spoof of *Dick Tracy*?

581) Wash Tubbs met a two-fisted friend who eventually stole his comic strip. Who was he?

582) In what way did Sinbad Jr. gain great power in his cartoon series?

583) Which member of the New Teen Titans is from the planet Tamaran?
   a. Cyborg
   b. Raven
   c. Lilith
   d. Starfire

584) Who leads the Uncanny X-Men?

585) What is the name of the police officer who tried to keep order in Top Cat's neighborhood?

586) Name the ship Beany and Cecil sailed.

. . . Answers

577. False, he was a skunk

578. Hans and Fritz

579. The Royal Order of Water Buffalo

580. *Fearless Fosdick*

581. Captain Easy

582. He tightened his magical belt

583. d

584. Professor Xavier

585. Officer Dibble

586. The Leakin' Lena

587) Where does the Phantom live?

588) Until recently, where did Doonesbury live?

589) In *Calvin and the Colonel*, what was the Colonel's full name?

590) What flower did Basil St. John require in *Brenda Starr*?

591) What was Alexander Bumstead's original name?

592) When Bugs Bunny was accidentally hypnotized at a sanitarium, who did he think he was?

593) Name the leader on *New Genesis*.

594) Buster Brown started in a comic strip. Can you name his dog?

595) Who was Mr. Miracle before Scott Free?

596) Aqualad is Aquaman's son. True or False?

597) An *Andy Panda* cartoon gave birth to a famous, cantankerous bird. Name him.

598) Bart Hawk became the leader of which flying squadron in World War II?

599) What is the Mad Thinker's usual downfall?

... *Answers*

587. Skull Cave, Africa

588. Walden Puddle

589. Montgomery J. Klaxton

590. A black orchid

591. Baby Dumpling

592. Elmer J. Fudd, millionaire, who owned a mansion and a yacht

593. Highfather

594. Tige

595. Thaddeus Brown

596. False

597. Woody Woodpecker

598. The Blackhawks

599. The unexpected "X" Factor

600) Can you name the adventurous penguin and walrus duo?

601) Batman's butler Alfred has a last name. Do you know it?

602) What did Dagwood give up to marry Blondie?

603) The Legion of Super Heroes have their headquarters in what city?

604) When Machine Man was built, he was officially designated as
    a. XL-5
    b. XYZ
    c. X-1
    d. X-51

605) Beany and Cecil were always at odds with whom?

606) *Devil Dinosaur* was about a boy and his red pet dinosaur. True or false?

607) When Tweety exclaimed, "I thought I thaw a putty tat," who did he see?

608) Who is the inventor with good intentions and bad luck in Superman's life?

609) Name the world's fastest mouse.

. . . Answers

600. Tennessee Tuxedo and Chumley

601. Pennyworth

602. He was written out of his wealthy family's will

603. Metropolis

604. d

605. Dishonest John

606. True

607. Sylvester

608. Professor Potter

609. Speedy Gonzales

QUESTIONS

610) What was the first Marvel comic?

611) Name the original Invaders.

612) Who is Koriand'r's (Starfire's) sister?

613) What came out of Milton's head?

614) Where did the Go-Go Gophers live?

615) Name the two blob members of the animated *Herculoids*.

616) Chalkie is Andy Capp's partner in mayhem. True or False?

617) Name the futuristic samurai epic Frank Miller did after *Daredevil*.

618) Which intergalactic Princess is the *X-Men's* Charles Xavier in love with?

619) Which *Flash* foe comes from the 64th Century?
    a. The Top
    b. Abra Kadabra
    c. Dr. Alechmy
    d. Grodd.

620) Name the renegade Green Lantern who is Hal Jordan's sworn enemy.

. . . *Answers*

610. *Marvel Mystery Comics*

611. Captain America, Bucky, The Human Torch, Toro, Sub-Mariner

612. Komand'r (Blackfire)

613. Steam

614. Gopher Gulch

615. Gloop and Gleep

616. True

617. *Ronin*

618. Lillandra

619. b

620. Sinestro

621) What stellar object does Ziggy talk to?

622) Give the full name of the reporter covering *Doonesbury*'s Walden Puddle.

623) Gadzooki has a large, green friend. Who is he?

624) Who is Alec Tronn's girl friend in the *E-Man* comic book?

625) Who was comicdom's futuristic robot fighter?

626) In cartoons, who was the world's richest teenager?

627) Opus the Penguin lives with which *Bloom County* resident:
    a. Milo Bloom
    b. Binkley
    c. Oliver Wendell Jones
    d. Steve Dallas

628) Frank Frazetta was an art assistant on *Li'l Abner*. True or False?

629) Name Marvel's humor comic which spoofed all comics.

630) Who is the stunt cyclist possessed by a demon in Marvel comics?

631) Name the man who took in and raised Skeezik in Gasoline Alley.

... *Answers*

621. The Wishing Star

622. Roland Burton Hedley, Jr.

623. Godzilla

624. Nova Kane

625. Magnus

626. Goldie Gold

627. b

628. True

629. *Not Brand Ecch*!

630. Johnny Blaze

631. Walt Wallet

632) Who is King in Alley Oop's home of Moo?

633) What was the last animated series Tex Avery worked on?

634) *Flash Gordon's* writer/artist Dan Barry is related to what other strip artist?

635) When Jessica Drew stopped being Spider-Woman, what profession did she resume?

636) Before becoming Tigra, what was the Chicagoan's true name?

637) On the *Kid Super Power Hour*, where did the fledgling heroes train?

638) Popeye was introduced in which comic strip?

639) Where does Clark Kent live?

640) Name four famous cartoon cats.

641) What does SHAZAM stand for?

642) The second Earthman to become a Green Lantern is:
   a. Charlie Vickers
   b. John Stewart
   c. Guy Gardner
   d. Hal Jordan

. . . Answers

632. Guz

633. *Kwicky Koala*

634. Sy Barry, artist of the *Phantom*

635. Private detective

636. Greer Nelson

637. Hero High

638. *Thimble Theater*

639. 344 Clinton Street

640. Felix, Krazy, Tom, Sylvester, Fritz, the Cheshire (Alice), Figaro (Pinocchio)

641. Solomon, Hercules, Atlas, Zeus, Achilles, Mercury

642. a

643) Can you name Alley Oop's girl friend?

644) What is Jungle Jim's last name from the comic strips?

645) Name Commissioner Gordon's two children.

646) Who has been the only voice for Donald Duck over the last 50 years?

647) Galactus is the sole survivor of:
    a. Taa
    b. Oa
    c. Lallor
    d. Gar

648) What happened at the end of each *Little Nemo* adventure?

649) Who supplied Buck Rogers with scientific assistance?

650) What is Supergirl's secret identity?

651) Before *Mickey Mouse* took off, Disney was known for a series of cartoons. What were they called?

652) Name Li'l Abner's favorite Indian drink.

653) Milo Bloom writes nasty editorials about which politician?

. . . Answers

643. Oola

644. Bradley

645. Tony and Barbara

646. Clarence Nash

647. a

648. He woke up

649. Dr. Huer

650. Linda Lee Danvers

651. *Silly Symphonies*

652. Kickapoo Joy Juice

653. Senator Lucius Bedfellow

654) What is the relationship between Mary and Billy Batson?

655) Tony Stark, Iron Man, ran what company?

656) Who always says, "Th-th-th-that's all folks!"

657) What is the Sub-Mariner's given name?

658) Which super-hero loves peace enough to kill for it?

659) Daddy Warbucks adopted which comic strip heroine?

660) According to the TV series, how far is Wayne Mansion from Gotham City?

661) Where does Yogi Bear live?

662) How does Wonder Woman control her invisible airplane?

663) Whom do the Green Lantern Corps report to in the DC comics?

664) Which Marvel comic book characters received their own comic strips?

665) Which TV series has never been a cartoon series?
    a. Happy Days   c. The Brady Bunch
    b. Gomer Pyle   d. Mork and Mindy

. . . Answers

654. They are brother and sister

655. Stark International

656. Porky Pig

657. Prince Namor the First

658. Peacemaker

659. Little Orphan Annie

660. 14 miles

661. Jellystone Park

662. Mental commands

663. Guardians of the Universe

664. Howard the Duck, The Amazing Spider-Man, The Incredible Hulk, and Conan the Barbarian

665. b

666) Who created, built, and runs DC's Ferris Aircraft Company?

667) Roy Harper, Green Arrow's ward, has kicked which bad habit?

668) Name Mandrake's arch-enemy.

669) The Phantom goes by what secret identity?

670) Who murdered the Flash's wife?

671) Why is Christopher Chance called the Human Target?

672) Name the European hit, now an animated series about underwater people.

673) The Jackson Five once had a cartoon series and provided the voices. True or False?

674) Who runs the Wayne Foundation now that Bruce Wayne has relinquished his duties?

675) Jean Gray was a member of the X-Men under two different names. What were they?

676) What was the first animated mini-series?

677) What was the name of B.B. Eyes's kid brother?

. . . Answers

666. Carl Ferris

667. Drugs

668. The Cobra

669. Kit Walker

670. The Reverse-Flash

671. For a fee, he will impersonate someone marked for death

672. The Snorks

673. True

674. Lucius Fox

675. Marvel Girl and Phoenix

676. *G.I. Joe — A Real American Hero*

677. B.D. Eyes

678) Who stole Ms. Marvel's memories and powers in the comic books?

679) Who was the first person to leave the New Teen Titans?

680) What was the premise behind cartoondom's *Sealab 2020*?

681) Other than Woodstock, name the four birds comprising Snoopy's Beagle Patrol hikes.

682) Whom does Alec Tronn, E-Man, work for?
    a. Mike Hammer
    b. Mike Myste
    c. Mike Tree
    d. Mike Mauser

683) The Princess in *Conrad* has an animal convinced it's a dog. What is it really?

684) Name the elixir that gives Elongated Man his powers.

685) Which Legionnaires were the first to marry?

686) What was the first made-for-television cartoon series?

687) Ziggy's psychiatrist is named Dr. Shrink. True or False?

. . . Answers

678. Rogue

679. Kid Flash

680. It was about an experimental undersea community

681. Conrad, Oliver, Bill, and Harriet

682. d

683. An alligator

684. Gingold

685. Duo Damsel and Bouncing Boy

686. Crusader Rabbit

687. True

688) Who is always trying to get the rent from Andy Capp?

689) Who was the original Blue Beetle?
   a. Ted Kord
   b. Dan Garret
   c. Charley Parker
   d. Danny Rand

690) When not Birdman, Ray Randall does what for a living?

691) Can you name Cathy's on again/off again boy friend?

692) Marvin is a:
   a. Frog
   b. Prince
   c. Cat
   d. Infant

693) Where is the Peacemaker's headquarters?

694) Who was Sgt. Fury's commanding officer in World War II?

695) How did Dr. Don Blake turn into the Mighty Thor?

696) When Mike Doonesbury arrived at college, who was his first roommate?

. . . Answers

688. Percy

689. b

690. He is a police officer

691. Irving

692. d

693. A chalet in Geneva

694. Capt. "Happy" Sam Sawyer

695. He thumped his walking stick on the ground, calling forth magic

696. B.D.

QUESTIONS

697) Where did George of the Jungle live?

698) Brenda Starr works for the *Daily Flash*. Name her competition.

699) Which Marvel mutant married which Inhuman?

700) Who was the last animal to join DC's Amazing Zoo Crew?

701) What generation is the modern-day Phantom?

702) Super Service Inc. featured for hire what super group?

703) Who leads the Legion of Substitute Heroes?

704) What does "DC" in DC Comics stand for?

705) Who was Dick Tracy's original partner?

706) Did Space Ghost's armbands have any significance?

707) Where did Mandrake learn his art?

708) What is the first comic to offer all-new material?

709) Name Dondi's adoptive grandfather.

710) Name the Galaxy Trio.

. . . *Answers*

697. Imgwee Gwee Valley

698. *The Globe*

699. Quicksilver married Crystal

700. Little Cheese

701. 21st generation

702. The Super Six

703. Polar Boy

704. Detective Comics

705. Pat Patton

706. Yes, they controlled his various powers

707. The College of Magic

708. Detective Comics

709. Pop Fleigh

710. Vapor Man, Meteor Man, Galaxy Girl

711) Name the two people who merge to become Firestorm.

712) Skyler, from the *Shoe* comic strip, is a whiz at what?

713) What do Crusader Rabbit, Dudley Do-Right, and Rocky have in common?

714) Dick Tracy had his own cartoon series and featured three operatives. What was the name of the Oriental one?

715) *Li'l Abner's* Al Capp wrote the introductory story for which legendary strip?
   a. *Abbie & Slats*
   b. *Rip Kirby*
   c. *Scorchy Smith*
   d. *Pogo*

716) There was once a *Mike Hammer* comic strip. True or False?

717) When not drinking, sleeping, or playing rugby, what else did Andy Capp do?

718) Where did Clark Kent attend college?

719) What special property does Wonder Woman's magic lasso possess?

720) How does the Elongated Man know a mystery is afoot?

. . . *Answers*

711. Ronnie Raymond and Prof. Martin Stein

712. Computer and video games

713. They were all co-created by Jay Ward

714. Ju Jitsu

715. a

716. True

717. Played snooker, chased women, and threw darts

718. Metropolis University

719. The lasso compels people to tell the truth

720. His nose twitches

721) Can you name the two long-running comic strips created by Lee Falk?

722) Did Walt Disney really write and draw the *Mickey Mouse* comic strip?

723) When Steve and Ellie Patterson took a dog home, what did they name him?

724) What were the names of the cartoon duo known as The Beagles?

725) When *Beetle Bailey* started in 1950, was it about the army?

726) In Marvel comics, name the planetwide computer within Jupiter's moon Titan.

727) Torin MacQuillon is better known as:
    a. Starjammer
    b. Starslammer
    c. Starslayer
    d. Starsilver

728) Who is the nebbish that is Marvel's official mascot?

729) Dawg is owned by which comic strip family?

730) Who is Westview High's star football player in *Funky Winkerbean*?

. . . Answers

721. *Mandrake the Magician* and *The Phantom*

722. He wrote some of the early stories but never drew the strip

723. Farley

724. Stringer and Tubby

725. No, it was first a college strip, and then he enlisted

726. Issac

727. c

728. Irving Forbush

729. *Hi and Lois*

730. Bull Bushka

731) Batman creator Bob Kane created what animated spy?

732) Mutt and Jeff were a famous comic strip team but what's Mutt's first name?

733) Name all three animated Impossibles and their animated super-powers.

734) Name Matt Murdock's first secretary who went on to be a movie star.

735) What did Warlock wear on his forehead in Marvel comics?

736) The dread Dormammu rules which domain?
    a. Earth-Prime
    b. Fifth Dimension
    c. Dark Dimension
    d. Dream Dimension

737) Who is Pogo's best friend?

738) Asgaard's Enchantress's real name is Sersi. True or False?

739) What gives Super Chicken his powers?

740) Simon Williams, Wonder Man, has a criminal brother. Name him.

. . . Answers

731. Cool McCool

732. Augustus

733. Fluid Man could turn to water; Coil Man could spring; Multiple Man could multiply himself

734. Karen Page

735. Soulgem

736. c

737. Porky Pine

738. False, it's Amora

739. Super sauce

740. Eric, the Grim Reaper

741) How did Samson and his dog Goliath become su-per-powered in cartoons?

742) Name the vessel used by Marvel's Guardians of the Galaxy.

743) In *Archie*, what is Moose's last name?

744) Radio broadcaster Vic Sage is also a comic book crimebuster. Name him.

745) How many floors make up the Fantastic Four's headquarters?
   a. 3
   b. 4
   c. 5
   d. 7

746) Who accompanied Space Ghost on his missions?

747) What is Crusher Creel, the Absorbing Man's first name?

748) Name Barnaby's fairy godfather in the comic strip.

749) A splinter group of Hydra is A.I.M. What do the initials mean?

750) Which comic strip character has been declared to have the lowest IQ in America?

. . . Answers

741. He slapped his wristbands together and cried, "I need Samson power!"

742. *Freedom's Lady*

743. Mason

744. The Question

745. c

746. Jan, Jace, and Blip the monkey

747. Karl

748. Mr. O'Malley

749. Advanced Idea Mechanics

750. Li'l Abner

751) Warren Kenneth Worthington III is also the Angel in comics. True or False?

752) Scooter, Snoopy, Countdown, and Jenny were better known as what cartoon team?

753) Arkon the Magnificent hails from which Marvel planet?

754) What is Andy Capp's chosen sport?

755) Name all of Ziggy's pets.

756) Who are cartoondom's Super Six?

757) Who is the Sub-Mariner's Vizier?

758) What is the hometown of Mark Scarlotti, the Blacklash?

759) We have never been told the name of the father in the *Family Circus*. True or False?

760) What god bestowed great power to Ray Randall, turning him into Birdman?

761) Judomaster is really Rip Jagger, but what is his army rank?

762) What is Wonder Wart-Hog's secret identity?

. . . Answers

751. True

752. The Space Kidettes

753. Polemachus

754. Rugby

755. Fuzz, the dog, Twerp the bird, and Wack the duck

756. Captain Whammy, Magnet Man, Elevator Man, Granite Man, Super Scuba, and Super Bwoing

757. Vashti

758. Cleveland, Ohio

759. True

760. Ra, the Egyptian sun god

761. Sergeant

762. Philbert Desanex

763) Ellie, in *For Better or For Worse*, goes to night school to take what subjects?

764) *Beetle Bailey*'s Sarge was once married. True or False?

765) What was the longest running prime time cartoon series?

766) Supergirl's Kryptonian name is:
   a. Kara Jor-El
   b. Kara Zor-El
   c. Kara
   d. Kara-Alura

767) To travel from Apokolips or New Genesis to Earth, what does one use?

768) Name the long-suffering columnist in *Shoe*.

769) Baby Huey was what kind of animal in cartoons and comic books?

770) Who lived in the sacred land of Moo, 50 million years ago?

771) Who was the first person to join after the Legion of Super-Heroes was formed?

772) Where do the Blackhawks maintain their operations?

. . . Answers

763. English and creative writing

764. True, but she was dropped from the strip

765. The Flintstones

766. b

767. The Boom Tube

768. Perfesser Cosmo Fishhawk

769. An overgrown duck

770. Alley Oop

771. Phantom Girl

772. Blackhawk Island, near England

773) Uncle Duke was named governor to what American province in *Doonesbury*?

774) *Fractured Fairy Tales* was narrated by which popular character actor?

775) How did Jiggs become a millionaire in the comic strip?

776) Andy Gump has one distinguishing feature. What is it?

777) Name the impish alien who befriended Fred Flintstone.

778) Which of the following is not a member of DC Comics' Easy Company?
    a. Wildman
    b. Bulldozer
    c. Ice Cream Soldier
    d. Tank

779) Jack Kirby once drew the original Captain Marvel. True or False?

780) Which legendary animator gave us Foghorn Leghorn and the Tasmanian Devil?

781) In Dogpatch, when can women legally chase the men?

. . . Answers

773. Samoa

774. Edward Everett Horton

775. He won a sweepstakes

776. He has no chin

777. The Great Kazoo

778. d

779. True

780. Bob McKimson

781. Sadie Hawkins Day

782) Where did Pogo live?

783) Who ruled the cartoon kingdom of Congo Bongo?

784) Can you name Captain America's original partner?

785) Name the original line-up of the Avengers.

786) Who created Alvin and the Chipmunks?

787) Flo Capp's best friend is:
   a. Rube
   b. Dolly
   c. Ducky
   d. Lily

788) What is acknowledged as the first comic book?

789) What is the Rawhide Kid's real name?

790) How did Space Ghost turn invisible?

791) In DC's *Camelot 3000*, everyone was resurrected. What did Tristan come back as?

792) Who was the Space Kidettes' arch enemy?

793) Who did the Phantom marry?

794) Of which country was Cerebus the Aardvark Prime Minister?

. . . Answers

782. Okefenokee Swamp

783. King Leonardo, a lion

784. Bucky Barnes

785. Iron Man, Thor, Hulk, Ant Man, and the Wasp

786. Ross Bagdasarian

787. a

788. *Famous Funnies*

789. Johnny Clay

790. He used his magic belt

791. A woman

792. Captain Skyhook

793. Diane Palmer

794. Iest

795) Power Man was once a member of the Fantastic Four. True or False?

796) Sally Struthers was the voice for which cartoon heroine?

797) Who was the Ancient One's disciple before Dr. Strange?

798) Who was the Spirit's most frequent, unseen opponent?

799) Which video game has yet to appear on *Saturday Supercade*?
   a. Dragon's Lair
   b. Q*Bert
   c. Kangaroo
   d. Frogger

800) In the comic strip, what is the Tiger's dog's name?

801) Name the guiding spirit in Deadman's comic book life.

802) What happens when the Hulk gets madder?

803) *The Amazing Chan* and the *Chan Clan* featured which detective?

804) Cain Marko, the Juggernaut, has a mutant step-brother. Name him.

. . . Answers

795. True

796. The teenage Pebbles

797. Baron Mordo

798. Octopus

799. a

800. Stripe

801. Rama Kushna

802. He gets stronger

803. Charlie Chan

804. Charles Xavier

805) Countess Giuletta Nefaria is the real name of Madame Masque. True or False?

806) The *Kid Power* animated series was based on what comic strip?

807) Name the daughter of Brenda Starr.

808) Who is Motley's best friend?

809) What is the Mad Thinker's usual downfall?

810) Who is Perfesser Cosmo Fishhawk's nephew?
    a. Billy
    b. Quentin
    c. Xavier
    d. Skyler

811) What is the full name of Beetle Bailey's sergeant?

812) How did the Kryptonian city of Kandor wind up in a bottle?

813) Name the three races unleashed by the Celestials in Marvel comics.

814) In the cartoon series, what was the Beagles' profession?

815) Ellie Patterson's friend, Connie, has dated which two men?

. . . Answers

805. True

806. Wee Pals

807. Starr Twinkle

808. Erle

809. The always unexpected "X" factor

810. d

811. Orville P. Snorkle

812. Brainiac used a shrinking ray to add it to his collection

813. Humans, Deviants, Eternals

814. They were singers

815. Ellie's brother, Phil, and Ted

816) Dondi's dog is named Freddie. True or False?

817) In the animated *King Kong*, where did the stories take place?

818) Who's the world's dirtiest witch in comic strip land?

819) To swing around town, Daredevil uses
   a. Billy club
   b. Devil wire
   c. Rope
   d. Hook and tackle

820) What did Darkseid seek, causing the Apokolips-New Genesis war?

821) Name Hi and Lois's next door neighbors.

822) Ted Cassidy was the voice for both the animated *Lurch* and *Frankenstein Jr*. True or False?

823) Where does Funky Winkerbean go to high school?

824) When the Eternals seek counsel, they merge into an entity. Name it.

825) Who did western gunfighter Johnny Thunder marry?

826) Who is Dennis the Menace's hero?

. . . *Answers*

816. False

817. Mondo, an island in the sea of Java

818. Broom Hilda

819. a

820. The Anti-Life Equation

821. Thirsty and Irma

822. True

823. Westview High

824. The Uni-Mind

825. Madame .44

826. Cowboy Bob

827) Angel Top is the daughter of which *Dick Tracy* villain?

828) When not fighting crime, what else did the Impossibles do professionally?

829) In *Bloom County*, what lurks in Binkley's closet?

830) A being called Him later took on the name:
    a. Starhawk
    b. Warlock
    c. Dreadstar
    d. Nighthawk

831) To command his magical thunderbolt, Johnny Thunder used what phrase?

832) What super-hero inhabited the *Bob Hope* comic book?

833) Can you name the only girl attracted to Jughead?

834) Name the Lockhorns.

835) What is the rallying cry in *Id*?

836) What is the name of Adam Strange's father-in-law?

837) Who is the Lord of Order, protecting the DC Comic's Earth from chaos?

. . . Answers

827. Flattop

828. They were singers

829. Anxieties

830. b

831. "Say You" or "Cei-U"

832. Super Hip

833. Big Ethel

834. Leroy and Loretta

835. "The King is a Fink!"

836. Sardath

837. Dr. Fate

838) Who edits the Bloom Beacon in *Bloom County*?

839) When Tennessee Tuxedo had a scientific problem, to whom did he turn?

840) Steel Sterling is followed around the country by what group of youngsters?

841) Robby Reed, who dialed "H" for HERO, had a favorite expression. What was it?

842) Which THUNDER Agent gave his life in the line of duty?

843) Whom do the Africans call the Ghost Who Walks?

844) What journalist can be found in and around Walden Puddle?

845) What planet do Hawkmen and Hawkwoman hail from?
    a. Rann
    b. Galador
    c. Mars
    d. Thanagar

846) What happens every time Lightning uses his powers?

847) How tall was the animated Frankenstein, Jr.?

. . . Answers

838. Overbeek

839. Professor Phineas J. Whoppee

840. The Young Steelers

841. "Sockamagee!"

842. Menthor

843. The Phantom

844. Roland Hedley, Jr.

845. d

846. He shortens his life span

847. 30 feet

848) Name Marc Spector's multiple personalities in the Marvel comics.

849) Who suggested three teens band together as the Legion of Super-Heroes?

850) What army officer has hounded the Incredible Hulk from the beginning?

851) Tom of THUMB was a cartoon governmental agent. What did THUMB stand for?

852) No one knows who the Black Orchid is. True or False?

853) What star-faring race brought about the Inhumans on Marvel's Earth?

854) In what city does the Spirit operate?

855) Name the children populating the *Family Circus*.

856) What is the name of Beetle Bailey's young brother?

857) What super-villain was responsible for Aquaman's son's death?

858) Where did Wile E. Coyote always get his devices?

859) Who created the Fantastic Four, Hulk, and Thor?

. . . Answers

848. Steve Grant, Jake Lockley, Moon Knight

849. R.J. Brande

850. General Thunderbolt Ross

851. Tiny Humans Underground Military Bureau

852. True

853. The Kree

854. Central City

855. Billy, Dolly, Jeffy, and P.J.

856. Chigger

857. Black Manta

858. Acme

859. Stan Lee and Jack Kirby

860) Name four people who died before becoming super-heroes.

861) What is the surname of Dick Tracy foes Flattop, Blowtop, Angel Top and Flattop Jr.?

862) Which Peanuts character often falls asleep in school?

863) Where does DC's Human Target maintain an office?

864) Name the Gotham police officer charged with maintaining the Bat Signal.

865) How many devices does Inspector Gadget have at his disposal?

866) Where does Crusader Rabbit live?

867) Before becoming Binary, Carol Danvers was a super-hero called:
    a. Raven
    b. Captain Marvel
    c. Ms. Marvel
    d. Starfire

868) Who leads the super-intelligent apes in *Gorilla City*?

869) Which rock star, in *Doonesbury*, gave up fame to return to college?

. . . Answers

860. Spectre, Deadman, the Gay Ghost, and Kid Eternity

861. Jones

862. Peppermint Patty

863. Boston

864. Sergeant Hainer

865. 13,000

866. Galahad Glen

867. c

868. Solivar

869. Jimmy Thudpucker

870) Blondie and Tootsie do most of their shopping at what department store?

871) Which *Flash* super-villains are brother and sister?

872) Name the family featured in the animated series *Roman Holidays*.

873) Which came first, the *Superman* comic book or comic strip?

874) Jack Kirby drew the strip adventures of which comic book hero?

875) Wonder Woman never had her own comic strip. True or False?

876) Which super-villain is Aquaman's half-brother?
   a. Ocean Master
   b. Fisherman
   c. Black Manta
   d. Shark

877) Can you name the strip created by Winsor McCay before *Little Nemo*?

878) Tex Avery stretched the limits of cartoon sexuality with which creation?

879) What is the fastest-growing comic strip of all time?

. . . *Answers*

870. Tudbury's

871. Captain Cold and the Golden Glider

872. The Holiday family

873. The comic book, although the strip was proposed first

874. Blue Beetle

875. False, she had a short-lived one in the 1940's

876. a

877. Dream of a Rarebit Fiend

878. Red Hot Riding Hood

879. *Hagar the Horrible*

880) Jack Hart was bathed in the Zero Fluid and became which Marvel hero?

881) What is the one person or thing loved by the Kingpin?

882) Harvey Kurtzman and Frank Frazetta never contributed to the *Flash Gordon* strip. True or False?

883) Name the inhabitants of cartoondom's Trolltown.

884) Name the vessel used by the Atari Force in the DC comics.

885) Ka-Zar was born in the Savage Land in Marvel's comics. True or False?

886) Who was the only person to know the 1940's Sandman's secret identity?

887) Who is the rightful heir to the throne of Mongo?

888) Who rules the realm of dreams and is Dr. Strange's sworn foe?

889) Name a canine cartoon character other than Huckleberry Hound to have a voice by Daws Butler.

890) Epic Comics' Coyote is part of which mythology?

891) Which Pepe Le Pew cartoon won an Academy Award?

. . . Answers

880. Jack of Hearts

881. His wife, Vanessa

882. False, they worked on one sequence in the 1950's

883. The Trollkins

884. *Scanner One*

885. False, he was born in America and stranded in the Savage Land

886. Dian Belmont

887. Prince Barin

888. Nightmare

889. Reddy of *Ruff and Reddy*

890. American Indian

891. *For Scent-imental Reasons*

892) Daimon Helstrom is better know as:
   a. Ghost Rider
   b. Son of Satan
   c. Satannish
   d. Dormamu

893) Who is the most charismatic of First Comics' Plexus Rangers?

894) Who serves lunch at Archie's Riverdale High?

895) Name the first super-hero team ever.

896) Why does Lex Luthor hate Superman?

897) Who was the first Legion of Super-Heroes member to die?

898) What is Li'l Abner's last name?

899) Which one-time director of Deputy Dawg went on to direct many animated feature films?

900) Who taught Matt Murdock to use his extraordinary abilities in Marvel comics?

901) Which member of the New Teen Titans is Trigon's daughter?

902) Although Tina always practices her tennis, what does Momma feel needs more practice?

. . . *Answers*

892. b

893. Reuben Flagg

894. Mrs. Beazly

895. The Justice Society of America

896. Superboy accidentally caused Luthor's hair to fall out, unhinging Luthor's fragile mind

897. Lightning Lad

898. Yokum

899. Ralph Bakshi

900. Stick

901. Raven

902. Cooking and cleaning

903) R. Rodney Rabbit eats a cosmic carrot and becomes which super-hero?

904) The 1970's comic, *Rima, The Jungle Girl*, is based on a novel. Name it.

905) Crock is about:
    a. The French Resistance
    b. The Underground Railroad
    c. The French Foreign Legion
    d. UNESCO

906) Snagglepuss was an announcer on which animated series?

907) Who is the youngest member of the X-Men?

908) What turned four Americans into the Fantastic Four?
    a. Gamma Rays
    b. X-Rays
    c. Cosmic Rays
    d. Ultra-Violet Rays

909) What is Dick Grayson's new costumed identity?

910) In the cartoon series, what is the name of Sinbad Jr.'s parrot?

911) What is the Penguin's real name?

. . . *Answers*

903. Captain Carrot

904. *Green Mansions*

905. c

906. Hanna-Barbera's *Laff-Olympics*

907. Kitty Pryde

908. c

909. Nightwing

910. Salty

911. Oswald Chesterfield Cobblepot

912) What kind of hat did Beany wear on the cartoon series?

913) Andy Capp has some form of employment. True or False?

914) How is the Flash related to Kid Flash?

915) Who was the voice of the legendary Huckleberry Hound?

916) Aquaman was a one-time King of Atlantis. Did he inherit the throne?

917) Who taught Doctor Stephen Strange the ways of magic?

918) What is a Schmoo from *Li'l Abner*?

919) Who is the Martian member of the Justice League of America?

920) What is Mr. Weatherbee's first name in the *Archie* series?

921) Which famous Warner Bros. cartoon director also contributed to *Tom and Jerry*?

922) Name the Green Lantern Hal Jordon of Earth succeeded.

. . . Answers

912. A cap with a propeller on top

913. False

914. Kid Flash is the Flash's nephew through marriage

915. Daws Butler

916. No, he was elected by the populace

917. The Ancient One

918. A boneless animal that wants to be eaten

919. J'Onn J'Onzz

920. Ainos

921. Chuck Jones

922. Abin Sur

923) In the Marvel series, Dracula married a woman. Can you name her?

924) Name Brutus Thornapple's mother-in-law.

925) King Vultan ruled which race on Mongo?

926) Which SHIELD agent died, leaving Captain America brokenhearted?

927) Epic Comics' Marada the She Wolf is a sorceress. True or False?

928) Who directed the first *Woody Woodpecker* cartoon?

929) Which is the only Dick Tracy villain to appear three times?
   a. The Brow
   b. Flattop
   c. 88 Keys
   d. Mumbles

930) Who protects DC Comics' realm of dreams?

931) Wes Dodds, DC Comics' first Sandman, took on a ward. Name him.

932) Who was the only member of the Doom Patrol to survive a bomb explosion?

. . . Answers

923. Domini

924. Mother Gargle

925. The Hawkmen

926. Sharon Carter

927. False, she is a mercenary

928. Walter Lantz

929. d

930. The Sandman

931. Sandy, the Golden Boy

932. Robotman

933) Name the duck trapped on a world he never made.

934) Who ran the Megopolis Zoo in the cartoons?

935) Quick Draw McGraw's partner, Baba Looey, was what kind of animal?

936) Opus the Penguin is running for Vice-President on which ticket?

937) Name the professions of the girls in Apartment 3-G.

938) What is the name of the unfortunate woman married to Andy Capp?

939) What device did Hawkman use to learn all Earth knowledge?

940) Which super-hero uses a Miraclo pill to gain super-strength?

941) When Archie Andrews becomes a super-hero, what is he called?

942) Name Hoppity Hooper's two traveling companions.

943) What does Charlie Brown's father do for a living?

944) For which paper does Brenda Starr work?

. . . Answers

933. Howard

934. Stanley Livingstone

935. A burro

936. The National Radical Meadow Party

937. Lou Ann is a teacher, Margo a secretary, and Tommi a nurse

938. Florence

939. His Thanagarian Absorbiscon

940. Hourman

941. Pureheart the Powerful

942. Filmore the Bear and Waldo Wigglesworth the Fox

943. He's a barber

944. *The Flash*

945) Name the cigar-smoking gangster who caused trouble for Underdog.

946) When not adventuring on Rann, what does Adam Strange call his profession?

947) Natasha Romanoff is better known as:
    a. The Black Widow
    b. The Black Cat
    c. The Black Canary
    d. The Black Condor

948) What speedster received his powers from mongoose blood?

949) Name the Go-Go Gophers.

950) Roz the short-order chef keeps the drinks coming for which *Shoe* cast member?

951) Have we ever seen Beetle Bailey's eyes?

952) What comic strip character had imaginary adventures while he slept?

953) Who was Batfink's cartoon partner?

954) What was atop Frankenstein Jr.'s head?
    a. Hat
    b. Antenna
    c. Propeller
    d. Satellite Dish

. . . Answers

945. Riff-Raff

946. He's an archeologist

947. a

948. The Whizzer

949. Ruffled Feathers and Running Board

950. Cosmo Fishhawk

951. Never

952. Dickie Dare

953. Karate

954. b

QUESTIONS

955) Who captained the *Leakin' Lena* in cartoons?

956) Who is student council president at Westview High in the comic strips?

957) In *Bloom County*, who captains the Wheelchair Enterprise?

958) What famous comic strip character died of acne?

959) Rita Farr married someone and together they adopted a boy. Name the husband and the boy.

960) What human fell in love with Howard the Duck?

961) Which emotion is an anathema to Man-Thing?
    a. Hate
    b. Jealousy
    c. Envy
    d. Fear

962) Where did Tennessee Tuxedo live?

963) To what organization did Klondike Kat belong in the cartoons?

964) In what city can you find Apartment 3-G?

965) Name the three girls who live in Apartment 3-G.

966) Where is SHIELD's main headquarters?

. . . Answers

955. Captain Huff-n-Puff

956. Barry Baldeman

957. Cutter John

958. Bill the Cat

959. Steve Dayton, Garfield Logna

960. Beverly Switzer

961. d

962. Megopolis Zoo

963. The Klondike Corps

964. New York

965. Lou Ann, Margo, Tammi

966. A helicarrier

967) Who is the most feared man in Mega City-One?

968) Name Nancy's Aunt in the comic strips.

969) Whom does Uncle Duke's girl friend, Honey, room with?

970) In *Elfquest*, what is Cutter's soul name?

971) Martha Halftrack, in *Beetle Bailey*, is taking tennis lessons from whom?

972) Hercules and his friend, Recorder, met a friendly Skrull. What was his name?

973) Name the cartoon series that introduced us to Mr. Magoo.

974) Who was the voice for Underdog?

975) How does Adam Strange journey to Rann in the comic books?

976) Name THUNDER's three top agents.

977) What cartoon series offered the talents of Sheldon Leonard, Carl Reiner, and Jonathan Winters?

. . . Answers

967. Judge Dredd

968. Fritzi Ritz

969. Joanie Caucus, Jr.

970. Tam

971. Rolf the tennis pro

972. Skyppi

973. *Ragtime Bear*

974. Wally Cox

975. Via Zeta beam

976. Dynamo, No-Man, and Lightning

977. Linus the Lionhearted

QUESTIONS

978) What is the Viking Prince's first name?
    a. Erik
    b. Arak
    c. Jon
    d. Fjord

979) Steve Dallas took Bobbi Harlow's relative to her high school prom. Who was she?

980) Funky Winkerbean accompanied which buddy to the National Air Guitar tournament?

981) Who are the Challengers of the Unknown?

982) Which member of the Legion of Super-Heroes has a mother who was President of Earth?

983) Thor and the Fantastic Four encountered a living planet. What was its name?

984) Who is considered Queen of the Jungle?

985) Name the dog in the *Chilly Willy* cartoons.

986) Captain America's arch-enemy is:
    a. Dr. Doom
    b. The Mandarin
    c. Red Skull
    d. Galactus

987) In the *Tom and Jerry* cartoons, what is the first name ever used for Tom?

. . . Answers

978. c

979. Yaz Pistachio

980. Crazy Harry

981. Ace Morgan, Red Ryan, Rocky Davis, and Professor Haley

982. Colossal Boy

983. Ego

984. Sheena

985. Smedley

986. c

987. Jasper in *Puss Gets the Boot*

988) Name the comic book heroine who took over her dead husband's detective agency.

989) In *Beetle Bailey*, can you name Sarge's dog?

990) When Terry Lee of *Terry and the Pirates* grew up, in which branch did he enlist?

991) Hoppy the Marvel Bunny says SHAZAM to get his powers. True or False?

992) Where did Sarge Steel get his metal hand?

993) Alec Tronn is an alien who came to Earth and became what super-hero?

994) Who is Sluggo's girl friend?

995) Who is Snoopy's brother?

996) Who created *Beany and Cecil* as a cartoon series?

997) Sinbad Jr. appeared on which cartoon series first?

998) Which members of the Howling Commandos joined SHIELD?

999) Who is the healer in the comic book *Elfquest*?

1000) Who brought together the original Doom Patrol?

. . . Answers

988. Ms. Tree

989. Otto

990. Air Force as a Flight Officer

991. True

992. After an accident in Vietnam

993. E-Man

994. Nancy

995. Spike

996. Bob Clampett

997. The Alvin Show

998. Dum Dum Dugan, Gabe Jones, Eric Koenig, and Nick Fury

999. Leetah

1000. Dr. Niles Caulder, the Chief

QUESTIONS

1001) What is Hi and Lois's last name?
   a. Flagston
   b. Flagg
   c. Flagstaff
   d. Flaggon

1002) Which cartoon character was known as the "Slowest Gun in the West"?

1003) Where did Snagglepuss first appear in cartoon-dom?

1004) What mythic figure does Linus Van Pelt wait for every year?

1005) Who loved Flash Gordon besides Dale?
   a. Aura
   b. Aleta
   c. Ardala
   d. Auron

1006) What is the name the deranged super-criminal Otto Octavius uses?

1007) Name the team Captain Carrot leads.

1008) Name the artist most associated with *Superman* for nearly 30 years.

1009) How long does it take for Spider-Man's web to evaporate?

. . . *Answers*

1001. a

1002. Quick Draw McGraw

1003. The *Quick-Draw McGraw* show

1004. The Great Pumpkin

1005. a

1006. Doctor Octopus

1007. The Amazing Zoo Crew

1008. Curt Swan

1009. 60 minutes

QUESTIONS

1010) What paper does Milo Bloom work for in the comic strips?

1011) Can you name Hi and Lois's children?

1012) Which X-Man was the first to formally leave the team?

1013) There was a radio show that lent its cast of characters and their voices to a Warner Bros. cartoon. What was the series?

1014) How does Superman get Mr. Myxlptlk to go back to the Fifth Dimension?

1015) Who is the permanent leader of the Legion of Super-Heroes' Espionage Squad?

1016) The Westview High Marching Band got to march in which comic strip parade?

1017) Gaylord the Buzzard hangs out with which filthy witch?

1018) To get around, what did the Atomic Knights ride on?

1019) What is the Silver Surfer's real name?

1020) In *For Better or For Worse*, John the dentist has an assistant. What's her name?

. . . Answers

1010. *The Bloom Beacon*

1011. Chip, Dot, Otto, and Trixie

1012. The Beast

1013. *The Jack Benny Show* pariticipated in *The Mouse that Jack Built*

1014. He tricks him into saying his name backward

1015. Chameleon Boy

1016. Tournament of Roses

1017. Broom Hilda

1018. Mutated dalmatians

1019. Norin Radd

1020. Jean Baker

1021) Uncle Scrooge McDuck first appeared in:
   a. Comic books
   b. Television show
   c. Cartoon
   d. Comic strip

1022) When the Guardian was cloned by DC Comics' DNA Project, what was he renamed?

1023) Which Canadian super-hero has admatium covering his bones?

1024) England's Modesty Blaise always works with a partner. What is his name?

1025) What Metropolis landmark was first introduced in the *Superman* cartoons of the 1940's?

1026) Who was Spacely Space Sprockets' competitor in *The Jetsons*?

1027) Who are Woody Woodpecker's niece and nephew?

1028) What is the name of Shoe's secretary at the *Treetops Tattler Tribune*?

1029) Who built Eighth Man?

1030) Simon Bar Sinister always threatened which cartoon super-hero?

. . . Answers

1021. a

1022. The Golden Guardian

1023. Wolverine

1024. Willie Garvin

1025. The globe atop the *Daily Planet* building

1026. Cogswell Cogs

1027. Knothead and Splinter

1028. Muffy

1029. Professor Brilliant

1030. Underdog

1031) Who owned the cat in *Josie and the Pussycats*?

1032) What super-hero did Tommy Troy become with the aid of his magic ring?

1033) Which comic book was not spawned directly from the pulp magazines:
    a. Doc Savage
    b. Shadow
    c. Batman
    d. Ka-Zar

1034) Which cats pursued Tweety Pie in in his first cartoon appearance?

1035) Who were Yankee's frequent enemies?

1036) Which Dr. Seuss creation won an Academy Award for its first cartoon appearance?

1037) Can you name the first television series produced by Hanna-Barbera?

1038) What was the name of cartoon hero Winky Dink's dog?

1039) Name at least one *Tom and Jerry* cartoon to win an Academy Award.

. . . Answers

1031. Alexandra

1032. The Fly

1033. c

1034. Babbitt and Catstello in *A Tale of Two Kitties*

1035. Fibber Fox and Alfie Gator

1036. Gerald McBoing-Boing

1037. *Ruff and Reddy*

1038. Woofer

1039. *Mouse Trouble, Yankee Doodle Mouse, Cat Concherto, Little Orphan, Two Mousketeers, Jonah Mouse*

1040) Which of the following is not a DC Comics locale?
  a. Midway City
  b. Midvale
  c. Ivy Town
  d. Rockland City

1041) Who evolved animals into near-human form in the Marvel universe?

1042) The *Doonesbury* crew made the cover of *Time* magazine for real. True or False?

1043) Which Peanuts character has a single-digit number as his name?

1044) How many color, "two reel" cartoons of Popeye did the Fleishers produce?

1045) Which cartoon character spoke in musical-instrument sounds?

1046) Where is Howard the Duck's real home?
  a. Duckburg
  b. Duckworld
  c. Duck Dimension
  d. Duckland

1047) What canary-yellow cartoon character was created by Bob Clampett?

. . . Answers

1040. d

1041. The High Evolutionary

1042. True

1043. Five

1044. Three

1045. Tom Terrific

1046. b

1047. Tweetie Pie

1048) To raise money for the 1984 Presidential campaign, Opus forged whose diaries?

1049) In addition to Hawkeye, Clint Barton has been another super-hero. Who?

1050) The 1940's Hawkman is actually a reincarnated prince from which ancient race?

1051) Many people helped create Bugs Bunny, but who gave him his definitive look?

1052) What is Wimpy's full name in *Popeye*?

1053) Which glamorous actress is a close friend of Dick Tracy?

1054) Name the lawyer for Heroes for Hire.

1055) Was Daffy Duck ever seen married in the cartoons?

1056) Geo-Force, of the Outsiders, had a super-powered half sister. Name her.

1057) What is Steve Canyon's full name?

. . . *Answers*

1048. Elvis Presley

1049. Goliath

1050. Egyptian

1051. Tex Avery

1052. J. Wellington Wimpy

1053. Sparkle Plenty

1054. Jeryn Hogarth

1055. Yes, to several different women

1056. Terra, Tara Markov

1057. Stevenson Burton Canyon

1058) Who is the one person Daddy Warbucks turns to for advice?

    a. Annie
    b. Mr. Am
    c. Punjab
    d. The President

1059) Name the two slave girls who aided George of the Jungle.

1060) When the Samson power was invoked in the cartoons, what did the dog Goliath become?

1061) Bram Velsing, the Dreadknight, is an exiled citizen of which Marvel country?

. . . Answers

1058. b

1059. Bella and Ursula

1060. A giant lion

1061. Latveria

ZEBRA HAS IT ALL!

PAY THE PRICE   (1234, $3.95)
by Igor Cassini

Christina was every woman's envy and every man's dream. And she was compulsively driven to making it—to the top of the modeling world and to the most powerful peaks of success, where an empire was hers for the taking, if she was willing to PAY THE PRICE.

PLEASURE DOME   (1134, $3.75)
by Judith Liederman

Though she posed as the perfect society wife, Laina Eastman was harboring a clandestine love. And within an empire of boundless opulence, throughout the decades following World War II, Laina's love would meet the challenges of fate . . .

DEBORAH'S LEGACY   (1153, $3.75)
by Stephen Marlowe

Deborah was young and innocent. Benton was worldly and experienced. And while the world rumbled with the thunder of battle, together they rose on a whirlwind of passion—daring fate, fear and fury to keep them apart!

FOUR SISTERS   (1048, $3.75)
by James Fritzhand

From the ghettos of Moscow to the glamor and glitter of the Winter Palace, four elegant beauties are torn between love and sorrow, danger and desire—but will forever be bound together as FOUR SISTERS.

BYGONES   (1030, $3.75)
by Frank Wilkinson

Once the extraordinary Gwyneth set eyes on the handsome aristocrat Benjamin Whisten, she was determined to foster the illicit love affair that would shape three generations—and win a remarkable woman an unforgettable dynasty!

Available wherever paperbacks are sold, or order direct from the Publisher. Send cover price plus 50¢ per copy for mailing and handling to Zebra Books, 475 Park Avenue South, New York, N.Y. 10016. DO NOT SEND CASH.